The Call of the Wyld
A Werewolf Anthology

Edited by:

Mark Bilsborough

Featuring:

Liam Hogan
Holly Rae Garcia
Christopher R Muscato
M T Johnson
Holly Barratt
Eric Nash
Laura Garrity
E J Sidle
C H Knyght
David Rank
Adam Stemple
Richard Pulfer

This edition published 2021 by Wyldblood Press, Thicket View, Maidenhead SL6 6PX

ISBN: 978-1-8381529-9-4

The Call of the Wyld

Paul Boswell

Contents

Introduction

When we started *Wyldblood Magazine*, back in that surreal Lockdown Spring of 2020, we had no idea that people would be sending us werewolf stories – by the truckload. Sure we had a cute picture of a wolf as a logo. Sure we had a slightly unsettling picture of a large and hungry pack of wolves on our masthead. Sure we took every opportunity to write bad wolf puns into every piece of advertising copy. And still the penny didn't drop. 'Hey, you're those werewolf people,' someone said on one of those rare summer days when we were actually allowed out to play.

'Er, actually we're a speculative and literary fiction publisher publishing everything from hard-SF to high fantasy.'

'And werewolves!'

Sigh. We *are* called Wyldblood Press, after all (it was my grandfather's middle name, in case you wondered. And he *definitely* wasn't a werewolf. I think).

We had to do something. And the best thing to do, obviously, was to double down on our unwitting werewolf obsession with this fine anthology – *Call of the Wyld*, home to all those moon inspired blood soaked wild descents into savagery and abandon we secretly craved.

Werewolves have been haunting people's dreams for millenia – waking hours too. The term lycanthropy dates back to the second century, used to suggest madness, but even earlier the ancient Greeks tell of savage man-like wolves (or is it wolf-like men?) Maybe it all started when the legendary King Lycaon tricked Zeus with a gory feast of his dismembered son and was (with some justification) transformed into a wolf by the vengeful god. And then there's *Little Red Riding Hood*, a werewolf lodestone if ever there was.

What's the appeal? Releasing the beast within us? The innate savagery of man? Something unsettling lurking in the dark? Thanks to Hollywood, werewolves and their legendary foes the vampires are now a ubiquitous part of our dark mythology, as gorily expressed in the *Underworld* films. The demon within is an enticing fantasy. And deep down, isn't there a bit of werewolf in all of us? No wonder we're entranced.

We open with Liam Hogan's *The Mortsafe,* full of gothic darkness, then swiftly through Holly Rae Garcia's *Werewolf's Lament* (because werewolves have feelings too) to Chris Muscato's *Howling on the Moon*. Werewolves in space – and right in the place where it all happens for them. Full moon all the time – kill or cure, right? Then M.T Johnson's *Ivanwolf* tells a very human story of some decidedly inhuman happenings.

To lighten things up, Holly Barratt's *Rabbit Ears in the Laundry* helps us face up to some of the more troublesome consequences of living with a werewolf, but the mood swiftly darkens as we follow up with the tense suspense of Eric Nash's unsettling *Rewilding.*

And the stories keep on coming. Laura Garrity's *The Lodger* explores what happens when the new guy in the spare bedroom suddenly has more fur than a landlady has a right to expect, followed by a tale of doomed love – *The Wolf is Always at Your Door* by E.J Sidle, and C. H. Knyght's *To Prey* which (spoiler) is nothing to do with going to church. We pause with the quirky *Walking Dog* by David J Rank before settling into a fine lupine love story – Adam Stemple's *Werewolf Eulogy*. We round off full circle with the *Big L* – like our opener *the Mortsafe*, this is a story of how to tame the curse, but with a very different outcome.

Our plan was to get werewolves out of our system, so we can concentrate on stories where we're not anticipating growling lycanthropes on every page we turn. But I've got a strong feeling, when that big old moon starts shining bright in a clear, crisp November night and something primal sounds distantly on the wind, we'll look at the dog stretched out on the hearth and wonder what his far distant cousins are up to.

And then we'll start to look for more werewolf stories.

These tales are best read by candlelight in front of a roaring fire. And keep the doors firmly bolted, just in case.

Mark Bilsborough
February 2021

The Mortsafe

Liam Hogan

His grip was like steel as he dragged me through the stonemason's yard. I'd been too bewildered to be properly scared, as Mister had marched along the busy thoroughfare, brushing aside startled pedestrians and weaving between clattering carriages. If I'd had longer to think about it I might have howled at the injustice; for nothing is crueller than to be vouchsafed a new and better life, only to have those promises dashed for reasons as yet unknown. To be dragged back to the narrow, twisting streets whence I had been rescued, with an urgency that took my breath away, and not to know *why*!

But it wasn't the dark, pungent alleyways, the tender underbelly of the city that feeds the insatiable factories and mills, to which we were bound. As the Gothic spire loomed into view, a soot-darkened needle against the tapestry of cloud and sky, I'd assumed the cemetery chapel was our destination and cursed him for a fool, for believing that a few prayers and a sprinkle of holy water could make a blind bit of difference. There are many who still think it would but I'd long been of the opinion that religion had nothing more to offer me since the day I had been ejected from its schoolrooms for being a girl rather than a boy, and I'd foolishly thought Mister felt the same, even if that might not always have been so.

Mister had already proven himself unlike any man I'd met in my seventeen years of earthly existence. So if his behaviour that spring day was unexpected and had come entirely out of the blue, I did not resist him the way I would certainly have done a mere month earlier.

After all, had he not saved my life? Had he not, in the intervening weeks, offered me more hope than I had thought existed? And yet my heart was in the polished shoes he had had me buy, fearing it was all about to end, that he had come to his senses and I was being cast out, that some irredeemable stain had been discovered on my soul, or perhaps worse, some steadily growing temptation on his part that only my immediate disavowal could head off. As we'd veered left and through the wide gate of the neighbouring mason's yard I'd fought in vain to escape his grip, the unknown scarier than what I could imagine. Being surrounded by half-carved angels and slabs of dark marble from which gravestones were ominously emerging did nothing to lighten my mood.

"I need a mortsafe!" Mister announced into the dust-filled gloom of the workshop as I caught my breath by the long table, littered with crumbs of stone and heavy chisels.

'Mister' was not his proper name, of course. The letters that came to his narrow townhouse were addressed to *Alfred W. Dunlace, Esquire*. Or, on very rare occasions, to *Reverend Dunlace*, though there was little evidence of this former vocation of his. He certainly didn't look the priest; tall and trim and always clean shaven. With a little more flesh on him he might have been mistaken for a well-to-do actor, though he had not their vanity; his suits were obviously good quality but hardly flashy, and none were new. I'd wondered if the letters were for a close but absent relative, a brother or even a father perhaps, though there was even less evidence for that.

Not long after I'd made his acquaintance and with my mouth stuffed full of bread and butter, I'd asked "What should I call you, Mister?" and he'd shared that odd grin of his and replied: "Mister will do, for now."

The grin was absent today and that unnerved me far more than the sleeping boneyard adjacent.

"What's a mortsafe?" I asked, rubbing my tender wrist as a weasel face popped up from behind a tall stack of marble slabs, narrow gaps between them where slats of wood kept them apart. Mister had let go of me by then, as if once we'd reached our destination he no longer had any fear that I might bolt.

If I had known...

"Perhaps, sir," the weasel faced mason began, peering at each of us in turn, "it would be more decent if the, um, girl were to wait *outside* as we discuss your business, to ah, prevent unseemly distress?"

"My *business*," Mister said, leaning on the word as though it was a weapon, "concerns the young woman, so she stays." He held the stonemason's gaze until it was lowered. It seemed a one-sided contest to me and how dearly I'd have loved to have the same presence, the same domineering effect, to inspire the same unthinking servility. A younger version of me had once thought it the consequence of the overly tall hat, but I'd come to be convinced it happened because Mister *expected* it to happen. I would have been as surprised as he had it not.

"Perhaps, however," Mister continued in a friendlier tone, now that the short battle was over, "you could do both of us a favour and answer the young woman's question?"

Weasel-face coloured as he dipped his gaze even lower. "Ah, sir, are you sure...?"

"Quite sure," confirmed Mister.

The stonemason gulped, took in a sharp breath that ended with his stifled cough kicking up a cloud of dust from the table. "Ah, well sir, a *mortsafe* is a heavy cage that is placed around a coffin or a shrouded corpse, for a week or so before the deceased can be interred in their *permanent* resting place."

I blinked. "What? Why?"

His eyes darted to mine, a flash of anger until he realised Mister wasn't about to correct my 'rudeness'. "I, um...?"

"...Because a fresh cadaver has value, Harriet, whereas a body even a week old does not." Mister helped out. "The mortsafe deters even the most ardent of resurrectionists." He turned his attention back to the waiting stonemason. "Do you have one?"

Weasel face wrung his hands together. "We have *several*, sir. The cost to hire is--"

"You misunderstand," Mister interrupted. "I do not wish to hire. I wish to purchase as solid a mortsafe as you have available."

"Sir?"

Mister smiled. "Perhaps you should fetch the foreman of this establishment, so that I might discuss the transaction with him?"

"Ah, yes, *certainly* sir. I'll fetch Mr Carson right away. Um, wait here, please?"

The mason seemed relieved to pass his unwanted responsibility to someone else, scurrying with evident eagerness to the even darker rear of the draughty workshop. I waited until I was reasonably sure he was out of earshot.

"Mister? Why does this concern me? I'm not *dead*."

I expected his easy grin to return and felt a pang when it did not. "Indeed not. Otherwise, a week's hire would be more than sufficient and considerably cheaper, I dare say. Especially as I doubt they get much custom for their mortsafes in these more enlightened times. The work of the anatomy inspectorate has made the effort of digging up even fresh bodies insufficiently rewarding for those so inclined. They will, I think, be more than happy to sell me one. Tell me, Harriet, does your wound itch?"

My hand flew to my arm, caught out by the sudden change of topic. I had hardly given it a thought this last week, but now that he mentioned it...

I'd acquired the twin crescent shaped scars on the foggy night Mister had come into my life. What an entrance he had made! Leaping from the darkness, a stout, metal-tipped cane raised high above his topper and flashing in the gaslight, driving off the beast that had attacked me. For it *was* a beast, for all that it had also been a man.

I had taken his intervention as a fortuitous diversion and ran blindly into the night, cradling my arm, leaving behind the tatters of my sleeve and my innocence. It hadn't been long before Mister caught up. I had been a fool to have put myself in the situation and I'd feared his authority almost as much as the attentions of that savage beast. If it were to come to light that I had attempted to *entice* my attacker...

And for what? A few lousy coins or even less; a meal to stave off the three-day hunger that gnawed at my stomach, a roof for the night.

Society does not look favourably on desperate girls such as I. But Mister, it turned out, had little truck with society.

Double fool that I was, I tried to thank my rescuer in kind, after he insisted that he treat the ugly bite mark on my arm, fed me, and offered me a bed to sleep in. Trembling with a mixture of relief and dread, I'd made it plain what I was willing to do in return.

In response he had laughed and grinned that grin of his for the first time. "I am not of that persuasion, Harriet. And besides, the cot I offer is rather too narrow for such endeavours."

I'd assumed one thing by his answer. Then another, the first time I heard him referred to as *Reverend*. And now... now I wasn't sure on either count. He had no particular eye for the young men we passed on the corners of certain streets, those that in turn had no eye for me, but nor did he pay any attention to their female counterparts. Passing an antiquarian or even a lowly hawker of penny-dreadfuls, on the other hand...

In the morning thin sunlight filtered through the tiny panes of the attic window and revealed the room at the very top of his house to contain nothing *but* books. Books, my narrow cot, and a beaten up but exceedingly comfortable armchair. More books than I had ever seen before, more even than I could glimpse through the dusty window of the bookseller I used to pass when I took the long way to the laundry I had slaved in since I was twelve.

I lingered for a while, cradling my bandaged arm and reading the spines of those dark and sombre volumes, imagining what thoughts, what bold ideas they might contain. Wondering too at my new and still unexplained circumstances, until I heard a distant clatter from below. Fearful that I had shown myself to be tardy I quickly descended to the kitchen at the very bottom of the house, where Mister had fed me a hearty breakfast.

And then we discussed--*explored*, he called it--my situation. "No point in rescuing a young women only to throw her back on the street!" he'd said cheerfully, though I'm not so sure about the truth of that sentiment either, in light of subsequent events.

"So," Mister said, towards the end of a long talk in which his silences had goaded me on to further and further confessions, "You would offer for a pittance to a stranger in the street that which you would not let your stepfather take in return for board and lodging?"

I'd angered at that. Flashed defiance, feeling heat on my checks and at my neck. How dare he judge me? But he wasn't finished.

"And would you have known what to do with him, had he shown you his coin instead of his teeth?"

The heat flared, as sudden and fierce as removing the tight fitting wooden lid from a boil wash. If he had smugly smiled I would have hated him; if he had laughed I would have killed him. Instead, his voice was surprisingly gentle. "I'll take that as a no. And Harriet, I am *glad*, on your behalf. Even a rumour of impropriety can ruin a person such as yourself.

"But perhaps we can find you a more profitable alternative to an abusive stepfather, to the inherent dangers of life on the street, or to the crushing misery of the workhouse. An alternative that demands nothing of you but your curiosity, your intellect, and your willingness to do the occasional task--nothing I hope too disagreeable--on my behalf. How do you like your attic room?"

Still flustered, I was unsure how to answer this aside. I had never had a bed all to myself before. A *room* all to myself. Even if it hadn't contained a single volume it would still have been a luxury beyond my expectation. As it was... "Have you read all those books, Mister?"

"No, not all. Many, yes. But a library without treasures still to be discovered would be an unhappy one, I feel. Can you read, Harriet?"

I scowled. "Of course I can!" And better than most, I was convinced, knowing the shape of letters even before my half-dozen years of schooling. Little good the learning had done me so far, firmly wedged between too little and too much, with no prospect of garnering more.

"Good, good. That'll help, greatly. Now, my library contains volumes collected over a number of years, from all corners of this world, and some of them are exceedingly rare. So if you are to make the attic your home then there are a few rules I would like you to obey."

I waited, heart sinking, certain I was about to be told I was forbidden from touching a single page.

"Firstly, I would very much appreciate it if you would return any books to the same position on the shelf that you found them. There is an order to the madness, even if it is perhaps not immediately clear.

"Secondly, and I would hope this mandate is unnecessary, but please treat the volumes with the same respect that I do, knowing I am only their *current* owner. With care they may have many others, in times yet to come. So, please, no bending of the corners--there are plenty of bookmarks you may employ--no cracking of the spines, no wax dripped across the pages, no scribbling in the margins."

He waited, as did I. He for my agreement, me for far more onerous restrictions. At last I gathered none were coming. "I can read any book I want?" I asked, astounded.

"What would be the point of a library where that wasn't true?" he replied, bemused. "Some you may need help to understand. Some of that help you will find in other books in my collection. Some works I may be able to assist you with myself, having trod the same path before you. Some, well... We'll find the assistance you'll need for those when we come to that point."

For the first time in a long while I glimpsed a future beyond the next day, beyond the next week. I'd left school five years earlier and was signed on at the laundry the same afternoon, marched from one to the other by my grim faced mother. I'd been convinced my education was at an end, that the path of my life had already been set, and set low. Despite being a Sunday School teacher until her great mistake--*me*--the only book my mother owned had been the family bible and I'd cried the day I'd come home, my hands red and raw, to find it gone, my smirking step-father having traded it for a half-bottle of cheap gin.

A fortnight later I'd run away, trying my best to fend for myself, and in so doing had almost become a tasty snack for a bedevilled mad-man.

And four weeks after that there I was, stood in a stonemason's yard, clutching a hot hand over the still livid bite mark gained that night. Was my unexpected idyll so abruptly at an end? Mister leant in close, his warm breath on my ear, voice husky. "What did I discover you eating, Harriet, before I stopped you, before I dragged you here?"

I jerked away, or tried to, confused. *That* had been my crime? "I was hungry. It was just a bite to eat... just cold beef..." I muttered.

He shook his head. "It was *raw* steak, Harriet."

The taste and texture forced its way back into my memory, buckling my knees. My teeth, grinding on fibres, metallic juices on my tongue and dripping down my lips, fingers dripping red. I stared down aghast at my hands, saw the brownish stains that remained.

I'd come down from the library ravenous, my luncheon delayed in favour of devouring another dozen pages, and then a dozen more, thinking that Mister must be gone for the day. But there had been other food in the larder that I had ignored; the remains of yesterday's mutton pie, half a loaf, a hunk of cheese. Instead, I'd found myself ripping the wax paper from that day's delivery from the butchers. It felt like a dream, like a nightmare, and yet there could be no denying it. And no denying the hunger was still there, lurking at the back of my mind, impatient and monstrous.

"The beast that attacked you," Mister said, speaking slowly, locking my eyes to his, "Is in your blood. You can sense it, can't you Harriet? Have you ever before felt this alive, this vital? And the feelings are only getting stronger as the moon waxes full. The infection is beginning to make its cruel demands of you. I'm afraid you have been cursed, or perhaps blessed. *That* will depend on your ability to control the urges."

My eyes filled with sudden tears. Tears, and questions. Questions I did not know how to ask. "Mister?"

He sighed. "I'm sorry, Harriet. I had hoped I'd be proven wrong, that you had been spared. And I let that hope delay my preparations far too long. We must take urgent action, *today*, for your safety and mine. The first step is the securing of a mortsafe."

I wailed. "But...but...but I don't want to be buried!"

"You won't be, I assure you. Now, hush. Here comes Mr Carson."

The price Mister paid for the mortsafe beggared belief. He'd ended up paying extra, once he'd expressed his preference for the one with an iron lid rather than stone, despite the weeds that grew up through the grill. But I'll give him this; he didn't grumble as he handed over the shiny sovereigns bearing the young head of the new queen. Though the cost did at least include delivery, which turned out to be far from trivial.

"I'm afraid," he announced as the mason's cart trundled up to the kerbside with its load, a pair of blinkered dray horses at the harness, "That there is no way we can get the mortsafe up the stairs. So, Harriet, for the next few nights at least, you'll need to bed down in my laboratory."

I must have winced, because he laid a gentle hand on my arm. "Don't worry. I have moved some of the more... *objectionable* items into temporary storage in the scullery. Perhaps I should henceforth call it the *skullery*, hmm?"

Mister only punned when he was nervous, a trait I hadn't pieced together until that moment, rare as those puns, and indeed his nerves, were. I couldn't muster a laugh in return. I was still slowly getting used to the idea he wanted me to *sleep* in the mortsafe. He hadn't fully explained why and I hadn't pushed him to do so, I was grappling with what he'd said about my being infected. Was I ill? I didn't feel it. Was I going to be? What illness would drive someone to consume raw meat?

There was only one I could think of and the thought churned my insides until I felt faint. Rabies. It would explain both my heinous actions and those of my attacker. It might even explain why I was to be caged.

But if it were so, why did Mister not *say*? Rabies would also mean certain, agonising death. Was Mister's reticence a kindness? I had no more faith in the doctors than the priests, had seen them execute cures more terrible than the symptoms for far lesser ailments. And rabies was a terrible, pitiful end, driven mad by phantasms of the mind. It would have been better to have had my heart torn out.

Throat dry, I retreated up the stairs between the ground and basement floor. I wanted to go further, even to my my attic sanctuary, but I couldn't. I had not the strength. I got halfway up that flight, to where the stairs widened and changed direction, and there I crumpled, peering through tear and snot dampenend fingers at the events unravelling below.

There was a lot of cursing as the men carried the mortsafe through to what was effectively the rear parlour, long since overtaken by yet more books, by shelves of ceramic and glass jars half familiar from the local apothecary, by display cases worthy of a museum, and by a workbench almost as long as that at the stonemason's. At some point, whether in Mister's tenure or perhaps predating him, the back parlour had been extended into the sloping garden behind the house, halving the underutilised space. Despite this extra room, the parlour was still crowded, the magpie habits of its current owner threatening to fill every inch. Some of the larger cases, artefacts, and tools had obviously come in to the house the same way the mortsafe did--winched down to the double-doors on the below-street ground floor, then carried along the wide corridor past the tucked away kitchen and the now cluttered scullery to the very back of the house.

It was a far from easy task, requiring the combined efforts of all six burly men, all busily ignoring Mister's helpful advice. The mortsafe came in two parts. The base was an iron cage, a little longer and twice as wide as my cot, though barely three feet high, with heavy-duty metal bars spanning the top, all welded together into one solid piece. And instead of a mattress the mortsafe lid was an even heavier slab of iron, perforated with diamond shaped gaps that made it look like an overgrown leaf from a monstrous tree. Mister had the men wrap chains around and through those holes, chains that arced up to a large wooden winch suspended from the ceiling. The two parts--the lid and the cage--locked together and were secured by four of the heaviest padlocks I've ever seen.

"I hope that's rated for the weight," one workman said, nodding at the winch as the lid swung noisily into place, flakes of paint raining down as the timbers above creaked and groaned.

"So do I," Mister replied, deadpan.

Mostly the men laughed and joked at the insanity of their task, trying to imagine why anyone would want a mortsafe in their parlour. But their humour was in short supply and the conclusions they reached soured their sweat-soaked faces. A few glanced my way, as I sat silently watching through the railings and into the parlour beyond. If I had said the right words, if I had accused Mister of some cruelty, some pending mischief, perhaps even if I had merely hid my head and wept, there would have been hell to pay.

The rest of the men looked for something large enough and valuable enough that anyone would go to such lengths to protect it. It was hard to identify anything worthy of the effort. Mister had a collection of curios, but did not appear to be a particularly *rich* bachelor, merely a middle-class, eccentric loner with a distinctly odd taste for graveyard furniture.

Mister tipped each man handsomely as they left, though few of them had the grace to thank him for it. An expensive days work. The narrow house lapsed back into almost shocking silence.

"Now, Harriet," Mister said, extending a hand. "Let us sit by the range and talk this through."

The kitchen had always been the cosiest of the rooms in the awkward four story house, the street some eight feet higher than the rear, such that the floors appeared out of true depending how far back into the house you went. The upper, street-level parlour was used for entertaining those guests who appreciated its formal primness, just about the only concession Mister made to polite society. The lower, back parlour, as has been mentioned and in common with pretty much the rest of the house, had been co-opted for Mister's eclectic studies. While my favourite room in the house was and always will be the attic library, it was best enjoyed alone, when I could idly pull from a shelf any volume that caught my eye, trying to gather as quickly as I could if it would be an interesting read or not, before I let the words swallow me whole.

Sandwiched between these were Mister's bedroom and dresser, and a small office where he attended to his correspondence. I had only ever seen those rooms briefly, on Mister's initial guided tour of the house, and had not had reason to revisit them.

We sat, then, on that lowest floor near the ever-ready range, with mugs of strong sweetened tea as though we were tradesmen, a loaf of fruited bread slowly reduced to crumbs between us.

"No Harriet," he reassured me as I gabbled my worst fears. "It is most definitely not rabies. It is rarer even than that unfortunate illness. But, god willing, you will not die. Do not let that sliver of good news blind you to how serious this is.

"The affliction--the *change*--is strongest at night, when the moon is full," Mister went on. I tried to picture what he was telling me as a fairy tale, tried to push away the dark thoughts by glancing up to the high windows, where the sun still shone on the street beyond. "The nights either side of the full moon can also be just as dangerous, especially if the full moon falls as close to one as to the other. And I've heard of a man who changed during the daytime, with the right provocation, though at great cost. So here is what I propose. It will not be easy for you and you may say no--"

I looked up with sudden hope, only for it to be just as suddenly dashed.

"--but I should warn you that if you do so, you will be on your own and my house will be barred to you, now, and forever."

I scowled. What sort of a choice was that? But still, I was tempted, as he described how I would be locked into the mortsafe, fed sparingly a strictly vegetarian diet, given a chamber pot and only allowed out for an hour around midday and only then if I had shown I was totally in control.

"Can't you just lock me in my room?" I whined, disconsolate. "Or if I have to be caged, could you not have acquired a roomier, animal cage, for instance? Rather than *that* morbid, cramped thing..."

He shook his head. In the half light of the kitchen it was impossible to see his eyes. "I'm sorry, Harriet. What you suggest *might* be sufficient. But I've seen it *not* be. I've seen the infected tear a normal cage apart, then scale walls and roofs. Only the weight and iron strength of a mortsafe guarantees your safety."

He sweetened the medicine by saying I could have all the books I wanted to read and even a pad to write on, but still, I did not enjoy the thought of being imprisoned in that metal relic, squatting unseen a couple of walls and a dozen feet away.

"And when," I said, staring at the tea leaves at the bottom of my mug and wishing I could see into my future, "will I have to enter the mortsafe?"

"Today. An hour before sunset. An hour from now."

I glanced up at the window. When had the sun gotten so low in the sky?

"I'm scared," I admitted.

"Don't be," he said. "You're safe. The trick will be to keep you so. I cannot be sure what will happen when the sun sets and the moon rises, even my library contains only passing mentions of what we face here and those reports are neither consistent nor *entirely* to be trusted, based on what I have witnessed for myself. And I may be being overly cautious. I hope so. But better that, surely, than under. Prudence is highly recommended when facing the uncertain, the unknown."

"You've seen this before?" I said, begging for scraps of comfort.

"Yes."

"Tell me, please!"

He shook his head. "I would prefer not to, not yet. There is no guarantee the course of the infection will be identical for you. Once we get through this, once the moon begins to wane again, then I will show you those reports and share everything I know, relate everything I have heard. But for now I ask that you trust me. Can you do that, Harriet?"

He held my gaze and I did what I could to calm myself, before solemnly nodding.

"Good. Then let us prepare for the night."

I helped haul on the chains until the mortsafe lid was suspended just above the cage. He locked it off, but still hung onto it, as if fearful it might slip. "Quickly now, Harriet. Into position."

Clutching the chamberpot I slipped between cage and lid, wincing as I banged my knee against one of the unforgiving upright rods. The cage didn't budge. The flagstone floor was cold and I shivered at that, and at the thought of being trapped there all night.

"Keep your fingers well away from the lid," Mister warned, as he lowered it into place, grunting at the effort to control its descent. The heavy metal slab clunked down and there was a screech as the mortsafe cut new grooves in the stone floor.

Mister passed a couple of blankets between the gaps. He pulled up a chair until his feet almost touched the flaking metal. And then he began to question what I had been reading most lately, what I had learnt. My mind was not on the task and he ended up doing most of the talking, recommending other books to read, different avenues to explore, names and titles I was confident I would never remember.

As he chatted away, the light of the day ebbed from the sky, the overgrown garden at the rear fading into the gloom. His conversation began to drift and the silence became so ominous I was about to beg him to relate more Pashtun tales about the backwards footed *Pichal Peri* of the mountainous Khyber. But before I could do so, Mister stood and in the near dark I saw him take up his wolf-headed cane and his darkest coat.

"You're not leaving me!" I begged, suddenly distraught.

"Harriet, I must," Mister said with sadness. "Making you secure is only one part of tonight's work. The return of the full moon means there is another of the infected abroad, one who has already shown himself incapable of mastering his urges. The streets are not safe."

"But..."

"Try to get some rest," he suggested and before I could conjure up a convincing argument on why he should stay he was gone, the soft sound as the parlour door shut behind him as final as that of any prison cell.

I folded one blanket beneath my head, wrapped the other both below and above me, and still I shivered. I'd slept in rougher conditions before, but never with so little hope of escape.

As my eyes adjusted, I explored the fragmented landscape beyond my cage. I was glad the skeleton that grinned in greeting each time I had previously ventured into the laboratory was temporarily relocated, though there were plenty of other horrors to haunt the night.

The mortsafe sat at the juncture of the old and new, original and extension, and the the beam that sported the block and tackle also supported an entire wall. Beyond it the roof of what had once been garden contained an expanse of glass and metal, the metal grill of the skylight echoing another mortsafe, though infinitely more delicate than the one I found myself in. Through the glass moonlight glinted, brighter than I had ever seen it. Or was it just the contrast, there being no other lights in the parlour?

I wondered at that. Why had I not asked Mister to leave a gaslight burning? Or even a candle? Had I done so, would he have refused? Weren't frightened animals best kept in the dark? Though what dark could there be on such a night as this. I stared up at that great bright globe, trying to work out if the moon was full and if not, how far away that was. Mister had said that it was still a day away, but it was hard to see the difference.

And as I stared, a thought, unbidden, sudden and terrifying, came to me. Only Mister had the keys to the padlocks, only he even knew I was here. What if some calamity befell him, out there in the treacherous night? Who would release me? Or would I perish here, my body only discovered long after, much too late, an unexplained and gruesome mystery that would forever blacken the former Reverend's name?

I found I was scratching my arm, at the rough edges of the bite. It wasn't painful and maybe it was because there was nothing else to do. Despite his earlier suggestion, I'd failed to gather up anything to read, perhaps for fear of making my stay here appear normal. I regretted that now, the moonlight was plenty bright enough and I had nothing to distract or engage my senses. I forced myself to stop itching, worried that I might tear the newly healed flesh.

The house, settling for the night and empty other than me, squeaked and groaned like an old tree in the wind. Something scratched from within the skirting board and I heard raised voices from the wall adjoining our neighbours, their layout presumably similar to ours, the argument punctuated by the sound of a meat cleaver falling onto a chopping board. At least, I *hoped* it was a chopping board. I'd never heard any noise from next door before tonight but then, I hadn't lain in an otherwise quiet house before tonight either.

I wondered what time it was. The moonlight from the window above tracked its way steadily across the floor, now lighting the large jars that sat on the lowest shelves. I tried to read their distant labels, but the names and worse, the abbreviations, meant little to me. *Sal* this, and *Lin* that. *Arsen?* I guessed that might be arsenic. They weren't enough to hold my interest for long.

I decided to recite my times tables. But my voice echoing through the cavernous room only reminded me of how alone I was and I couldn't bear to continue.

Eventually I guess I must have slept. Fractured dreams of running, through woods and along streams, the landscape brilliant white, as if covered in snow. Of being chased? No... there were no backwards glances, no *fear*, merely anticipation. I'd been searching for something, though I had no idea what.

I woke stiff necked when Mister returned in the early morning, the sky kissed by pink. "No luck," he said, looking as haggard as I felt, his beard an unaccustomed dark shadow on his angular chin. "No scent of the beast where you were attacked. Perhaps tonight..."

He scrutinised my position in the cage. I'd curled up like a child at one end, the blankets tucked around me. I didn't want to stretch out, to lie flat and be mistaken for a corpse. I'd pushed the used chamberpot to the other end of the confined space.

"And you, Harriet? How faired your night?"

I wished I'd listened more diligently when my step-father had cursed me out. I'd had plenty of opportunity. I'd have liked to use a few of his choicest words then.

"I solved the Irish Question," I claimed instead, driven to boldness.

"Oh?" He raised an eyebrow.

"But I'm afraid I clear forgot the solution. Is that really a full bottle of arsenic you have on your shelves?"

"Where?"

"Oh," I squinted. In the growing daylight I could hardly see the labels at all. "I must have only dreamt I could read them."

"Perhaps. The dark *does* play strange tricks on the imagination."

"Well?" I said, rapping hard against the iron lid, wincing as my knuckles came off the loser. "Are you going to let me out?"

"No. Not *quite* yet, Harriet." He crouched almost at my level, tilting his head back and forth, peering not at me but at my prison.

"What are you doing?"

"Looking for scratch marks."

I scoffed. "The lid and cage are solid iron, Mister!"

"Yes. And iron *does* seem to have a dampening effect. Much more so than silver, that doubtful legend of old, though perhaps if I could afford a cage this robust and made of solid silver it might be equally effective. Still, the mortsafe appears to have done its job. Are you hungry, Harriet?"

I nodded vigorously. I'd not eaten since yesterday, since the fruit loaf and tea. A flask that had contained water lay empty next to the chamberpot. "Starving!"

And then I remembered the meat and wished I could bite back my reply.

"Hmm. Show me your hands, please."

Eager to make amends, I stuck them through the lid of the mortsafe. Mister jerked as though scalded, before bending slowly back, eyeing me warily as he scrutinised my dirty nails. "Turn them over."

I did as I was asked and felt two cool fingers rest briefly on my wrist, gauging my pulse. He let go.

"Now, open your mouth? And bare your teeth."

Again, I did as I was instructed. "I'm not sure what you expect to see, Mister. I feel *fine*, if cold and stiff."

"I'm sure you do. Well, tonight will be the true test. But for now I think we're safe. We'll let you out, until sunset. Though I'll be wanting to keep an eye on you, so no disappearing up to the library, I'm afraid."

I took the chamberpot to the tiled water closet one level up, the indoor toilet a luxury I was becoming far too accustomed to. And then I slipped quietly upstairs, grabbing some warmer clothes. I patted the mattress on what I firmly thought of as my cot and wished I could sleep there that night.

Down in the kitchen I found Mister leafing through a stack of the morning's papers rather than the usual science and medicine journals. "Make yourself useful," he said, as he poured a cup of tea, pushing the *Gazette* my way where it lay next to a hunk of plain bread; no butter, cheese, or indeed anything else.

"What am I looking for?" I asked, tearing a small piece from the slice, doing my best not to wolf it down.

He peered over his cup. "Attacks. Grisly murders, though I think *they'd* be near the top of the news. Also, odd sightings, near scares. Anything that might indicate that there was a beast abroad last night, and most importantly, *where*."

It was dull work and in the end Mister was the one who found the report. He'd been reading a newspaper I'd already discarded, which peeved me somewhat until he drew my attention to an account I'd glossed over.

"Ah! Something here. A courting couple enter a graveyard late at night, but the young lady gets understandably spooked and rushes out into the arms of a night watchmen, claiming that someone--or *something*-- was after her, though she didn't see or indeed hear them. According to this, she is currently being treated for her nerves."

"So?" I ask. It seemed the thinnest of reports, merely two paragraphs long hidden towards the back of the paper.

"Suspicious, is it not, that no further mention is made of the young lady's companion?"

I looked down at the plate that still hovered by my elbow, wishing it wasn't already licked clean. "You think this young man was my assailant?" I asked, doubtful.

"No, Harriet. I think this young man has gone missing, but no-one has got round to reporting it yet. Hmm. I think I will begin my search in that neighbourhood, tonight."

I sighed. I had been trying to put thought of a repeat of yesterday's lonely vigil as far distant as possible. Mister paused a second.

"Do you want a challenge, Harriet? If you succeed, we may be able to dispense with the mortsafe altogether."

I nodded, though if I could dispense with it *tonight*, I'd have been even eager. At least Mister was offering me some future respite.

"With your permission, I'm going to leave a chunk of that raw meat you found so attractive, just beyond the bars. Within reach and easily retrieved, if you have the desire. *But* if you can control those urges, resist temptation, then I think we can trust you even during the next full moon."

I chewed on that for a moment. My empty stomach chimed in its contribution. "And... if I can't?"

He shrugged. "Then at least we know where we stand. The fault will not be yours, but that of the infection that lurks in your blood. And discipline you may not currently possess can assuredly be taught. Either way, Harriet, I am not about to desert you. Have no fear of that."

Small comfort as all too soon the heavy iron lid was lowered over me once again. As before, Mister kept me company as I settled but once again, as darkness prevailed, he bid me farewell, his last act placing that promised cut of raw beef a foot outside the cage. I wanted to tell him that it would be rotten by morning, a terrible waste, though in truth the parlour floor couldn't have been much warmer than the kitchen larder.

The thought of it, lying there, wasn't tempting at all.

Until the moon rose, shining down on my cage, without the faintest wisp of a cloud to soften the light, fuller even than before.

Something growled and I realised it was me. It wasn't fair! I'd been effectively starved, nothing but water and bread all day. Of course I was hungry!

Though even I realised I shouldn't be hungry for raw steak.

I retreated to the other side of the mortsafe. Turned my back on the meat that I could almost *hear* oozing red juices.

As I lay there, trying not to move, a small black shape shuttled around the edges of the slanted rectangles of moonlight. A mouse. It stopped, whiskers twitching, sniffing the air. Something froze it in its tracks. Was it the meat?

In a flash it reversed direction and I heard tiny claws clatter on the flagstones as it ran in desperation for the tiny gap it had only just emerged from.

Or was it *me*?

It seemed like the whole room was both alive and simultaneously holding its breath, ready for something to snap, waiting for something to erupt. Spiders held themselves in readiness, webs half spun, fearful to continue their nightly work. In the garden beyond, a pair of mirrored eyes stared my way as their owner stood static, before the fox--gravid with a new season's litter--executed an pre-rehearsed manoeuvre, leaping from abandoned wheelbarrow to low, ornamental wall to the ivy-covered nine feet high fence that separated us from our neighbours, briefly silhouetted as it checked for pursuit before vanishing to safer haunts.

I wasn't sure what was more remarkable, that these creatures of the night were so painfully aware of me, even though I lay immobile and incapable of venturing more than a couple of feet in any direction, or that I was aware of *them*. Though the moon was full, it surely wasn't bright enough to see everything at such a distance, yet everything was what I saw.

And felt, in vibrations that rippled through the solid stone floor. And heard, be it in the parlour, or next door, or outside.

And *smelt*...

Barely a body length away that piece of meat sat, out of sight but very, very present. My stomach fluttered at the thought and my fingers curled into claws. How *dare* Mister imprison me here? I'd eat that accursed meat just to spite him!

But, as I scuttled across my cage, it was the memory of the beast that had attacked me that sprung to mind, the way he had moved, his body twisted from the norm, arms bent more like legs, his neck long and narrow and his jaw jutting, cords of muscle writhing beneath the surface, the flash of insane light in his yellowed eyes as he lunged at me...

I was no beast.

Slowly, I retreated back to the other end of the mortsafe, my eyes locked on the wax parcel as though wary it might at any moment grow legs and instead come hunting for me.

I was still sitting there, having not slept a wink, when a gentle rain pattered on the parlour skylight and I looked up to greet a new, grey day. I was still sitting there when Mister staggered through the door, looking like it was holding him rather than he it. He glanced at the untouched parcel beyond the bars, glanced at me, rigid with grim determination, and nodded. His cane clattered to the floor, leaving a dark stain where it lay.

"The beast that attacked you is no more."

There was something different about him; I tried to latch onto it. Something... about the way Mister smelled. But the mortsafe, the metal that surrounded me, even that chunk of bait, no longer as fresh as when it had first been bought, a rancid tang that would have a housemaid wrinkling her nose, these all conspired to dull my senses. Whatever it was lurked just beyond my understanding. I eyed him with suspicion. What was he not telling me?

"The young man who disappeared?" I asked, fishing for clues.

He shook his head and I realised once again how lucky I had been to escape with only a bite, terrible though the consequences of that might be. How much worse would it be were it not for his arrival!

"Congratulations, Harriet," he said, slumping to his chair. "It seems your mission also met with success."

I was confused for a minute, thinking he too was talking about that night a month earlier. But then I remembered his promise: if I resisted the meat then I would not need to ever again spend my nights in the mortsafe.

The thought terrified me. Only I knew how close I'd been to giving in to the urge the raw meat had sparked. "But what if next full moon I fail? The *infection*... how can you be sure I can control it?"

"I can't," he said, slipping out of his ruined coat, rents gaping through the dark fabric, matching reddened marks on his shirt. "Fifteen years ago I was. Sure about *everything*. And if I was uncertain, then I was convinced I knew exactly where I'd find the answers. But I was wrong, very wrong. I learnt that the hard way, on my own."

He pulled up his shirt sleeve, brandishing his wiry arm. An ancient wound puckered the skin close to the elbow. A wound in the shape of a crescent. A wound like mine.

"Together Harriet," he said. "We'll get through it *together*. Now, let's get you out of that mortsafe."

Liam Hogan is an award winning short story writer, with stories in Best of British Science Fiction 2016 & 2019, and Best of British Fantasy 2018 (NewCon Press). He's been published by Analog, Daily Science Fiction, and Flame Tree Press, among others. He helps host Liars' League London, volunteers at the creative writing charity Ministry of Stories, and lives and avoids work in London.

More details at happyendingnotguaranteed.blogspot.co.uk

A Werewolf's Lament

Holly Rae Garcia

Listen to the silence. Engorged on a future that will never be, it permeates the air around you as you kneel at her grave.

It speaks of moonlit walks along the canal, hands clasped tightly.

It speaks of a first kiss, stolen in the shade of the oak tree behind her mother's house.

It screams of a dream's abrupt death.

These moments whirl around you as you crouch in the eye of the silent storm and regret the actions that led you both there. Her, cold and rotting in a cheap wooden casket beneath the ground. You, alone.

She was too good for you, you know this. You've always known this. But somehow, through Cupid's misplaced arrow, she loved you back. You tried to warn her, but she would laugh that beautiful laugh of hers. Her chestnut eyes would light up, and you would forget every reason you had to push her away. Of course she always thought you were joking, but you never joked about the darkness inside of you.

If she had only listened, she would still be alive. Gorgeous Victoria, with skin like fresh milk and hair black as a moonless night. She was beautiful even in death. The most beautiful woman you had ever known.

You managed to beat it for years, locking yourself in a steel cage on nights with a full moon under the guise of working late. But doubt had crept in, and you knew she wasn't buying it anymore. She thought there was another woman, as if you could ever love someone the way you loved her. The truth was much worse than any sordid affair.

She followed you that fateful night, down into the dungeon. You were so obsessed with getting there in time, you didn't hear her small footsteps behind you. Once inside the cage, you dropped the key in a box by the door that only a human hand could reach into, and sat down among the spider webs to await your fate. How were you to know she was watching from the shadows?

When she appeared you yelled at her to stay back, but she slipped her slender arm through the bars and into that box with the key. Ignoring your pleas, she pulled the key from its hiding place and into the lock hanging from the gate. There were eleven links in the chain and each one hammered a nail into your heart as they clattered to the ground.

You scrambled to put the chain back and to close the lock, but your inhuman hands had stopped obeying your human mind. Your fingers dropped the key as long claws protruded from your nails.

You'll never forget the look on her face when you turned towards her with a snarl. Or the way her screams cut off when you ripped into the flesh at her soft throat and you knew you'd never love another.

The storm of loss rages there, at her grave. And you are silent.

Holly Rae Garcia is a photographer and author on the Texas Coast. Her debut psychological thriller novel, Come Join the Murder, released March 2020. Her horror novella co-written with Ryan Prentice Garcia, The Easton Falls Massacre: Bigfoot's Revenge, releases Oct. 30th, 2020. She is also the Editor-at-Large and Art Director for Versification, an online micro poetry

magazine. Her other short fiction and poetry has been published online and in print.

More info can be found at _www.HollyRaeGarcia.com_

Howling on the Moon

Christopher R. Muscato

"You need to tell them."

"They didn't ask."

"So you didn't tell? This is different."

"It's personal. My business."

"Carlo, please. Please."

"What I am even supposed to say? Lo? Lo, can you hear me? Worthless piece of…" Carlo cursed at his phone, turning the offending device over in his hand. He held it up, searching for a signal. Everything humanity had achieved, colonies on the Moon, Mars, and still his phone dropped calls out here. He growled under his breath and shoved the phone into his bag. He'd call Lola back later, after his hunting trip. His last one, if everything went according to plan. With a glance towards the sky, he shouldered his pack and trudged off into the woods. There was a rhythmic haste to his march as Carlo disappeared into the brush. He wanted to get camp set up before the Sun set, and the Moon rose.

"Was it a good hunt, at least?" Lola asked, arms crossed. Carlo shrugged a cooler onto the counter, then leaned over and kissed her cheek, making it as slobbery as he could manage. She swatted him away, but couldn't conceal the twitch at the corners of her lips.

"Productive," Carlo answered her. "There's elk meat in the cooler, should be enough to last us until we leave."

"We'll savor it," Lola said, her tone shifting under the palpable tension hanging over the conversation. "I don't expect they'll have elk where we're going."

The meat was stored and supplies from the trip unpacked. Carlo and Lola found themselves huddled around a small fire, burning old papers and leaves on the property behind their house, the real estate agent's sign in their yard swinging in the night breeze. Lola shifted, settling into Carlo's shoulder as he wrapped a blanket around them both. She ran her fingers absentmindedly through his long, smooth locks, then sat up a little as her hand came away holding a small tuft of hair that was grey, coarse, and wiry. She tossed it aside, sighing, and the two of them looked up at the young moon.

"I'll miss it," she said softy. Carlo only replied by shooting her a pointed look with one eyebrow raised.

"You know what I mean." She rolled her eyes. "Miss seeing it. Like this."

Lola leaned over and glanced up at Carlo. He nodded, still silent, his eyes fixed on the shimmering crescent in the black sky.

Primary ignition.
We are go for launch.
And launching in T-minus 10, 9, 8…

Carlo gripped his seat through thick gloves, his helmet fogging slightly from his increased breathing as the shuttle roared to life, groaning and creaking as it shook loose the tethers of gravity. He felt the pressure of liftoff against him, pinning his head against his seat, but managed to force his eyes open long enough to glance over at Lola in the seat next to him. Her eyes were squeezed shut and lips pursed like she was holding back a scream.

"In two days, we will arrive at Lunar Colony Leto. There, you will be assigned habitation units and trade areas until such time as you can carve out a niche for yourself. The

Moon is a vital station for trade and supply ships, and your work here will help humanity push further into the stars. For many of you, this is also a chance to start over, build a new life. I know you all have your own reasons for leaving Earth, and we hope you will thrive here. We hope you find what you're looking for."

The group captain finished his introduction with a salutation, leaving the colonists to rumble excitedly amongst themselves. Carlo leaned in towards Lola, who was still looking a little green.

"We did it. We actually did it."

She nodded, eyes again squeezed shut, massaging the back of her neck with a clammy hand.

"You think it will work?"

Carlo felt his cheeks and ears start to burn and he instinctively glanced from side to side, shrinking slightly into the collar of his space suit, checking for eavesdroppers. Carlo gulped, his mouth dry. It had to work. He couldn't take it any longer. He just couldn't.

The shuttle hovered for a moment, then touched down on the launch pad with a tremendous thud. They had arrived. The airlock was secured and the colonists, helmets on for safety, departed the ship and took their first steps into their new home. Carlo squeezed Lola's hand through the cumbersome gloves as they traversed a narrow tunnel, passed through another airlock, and finally entered the great dome at the center of the colony. Through the radiation-shielded panels along the upper half of the dome, a thousand stars shimmered like living crystals, their light unimpeded by atmosphere or pollution. Dominating this extraordinary scene, however, was the big blue planet just rising into view. Longtime residents of the colony nudged each other and chuckled as the newcomers gasped and pointed at the sky. Lola's eyes, however, were transfixed wide and unblinking on Carlo. She bit her lip as he closed his eyes, basking in the glow of the Earth and the stars, and took a slow, purposeful breath. Then he opened his eyes, looked squarely at Lola, and a grin appeared on his face. He nodded. An enormous smile broke over her expression and she squeezed his hand, tears welling in the corners of her eyes.

"Honestly, I half expected it to backfire."

"You thought I'd…what? Explode?"

"In a manner of speaking," Lola confessed, snuggling up to Carlo, limbs overlapping. The habitation pod wasn't exactly spacious, but the coziness provided a nice comfort against the surrounding coldness of space.

"It's just," she continued, "there can be famously disastrous consequences for people who try to shirk a family curse. Literature is replete with examples."

"Works of fiction, you mean? Fairy tales."

"That's rich, coming from you."

Carlo shuffled uncomfortably, the burning in his ears returning. Lola kept talking.

"I only saw there being two likely outcomes, each as possible as the other. First was that it would work, like we hoped."

"And the other was that I'd explode?" Carlo's tone was amused, mocking.

"Either everything is possible or nothing is. Equally."

Carlo sighed and settled into his pillow, his mind replaying their conversations. Escape to the Moon. It's the only way. He thought back to the first time it happened. He still remembered it. He remembered every time. Each one was seared into his mind.

Lola leaned deeper into him and was soon asleep. Carlo, however, remained awake for quite some time that night, his wide eyes scanning the infinite stars, counting them, praying on them for salvation. He'd done it many times before. Maybe this time it worked.

"Benandanti, Carlo and Lola."
"Present."
"And accounted for."
"This way please."
Carlo and Lola followed the commander to his office, ready to receive their weekly assignments. The first few hadn't been so bad. The commander shuffled a stack of loose papers in the cramped workspace, artificial lights blinking dimly overhead.

"Alright, Mr. Benandanti it looks like we have you in the greenhouse, and Ma'am, kitchen detail. I know you're used to working together," he commented as Lola opened her mouth in protest. "We do try to keep couples assigned with each other, but that's just how it fell this time. Next week you'll be back on the same schedules. You're dismissed."

As they returned to their hab to get ready for work, Lola eyed Carlo cautiously.

"You'll be okay?"
"Why wouldn't I be?"
"The greenhouse doesn't have the same panels as the other domes; light and radiation are different in there."
"Lola, we've been on the Moon for a month. If it was going to happen, I think it would have by now. Relax, we did it. Just go enjoy kitchen duty."

Lola swatted at Carlo playfully, although she still felt a clear anxiety tugging at her chest.

"First time in the greenhouse?"
"Yeah," Carlo shuffled his basket as his fingers worked through the cauliflower beds. The woman across from him leaned against a trellis.

"You don't have to wear all the protective gear in here. I know more of the dome is exposed and everyone thinks the radiation is so different, but it's really not."

Carlo just nodded politely, keeping his attention on the crops. The woman shrugged.

"Alright, you're the cautious type. I get it." She paused. "Want to see something great, though?"

Carlo lifted his head, one eyebrow raised in curiosity. The woman gestured to him and he slowly set down his basket, following her deeper into the greenhouse. Carlo glanced up and noticed the steep sloping of the roof. They were nearing the edge of the greenhouse dome. Finally, the woman pulled aside a patch of foliage.

"Check this out," she waved him forward. Carlo felt the hair on his neck start to raise, beads of cold sweat forming. Behind the anxiety, however, he felt something else as well. Something beyond his control, something ancient, an instinct buried deep within him, pulling at him. One foot moved. Then the other. Carlo approached the paneled dome wall, not really sure why he was so compelled to do so.

"Pretty great, right?" The woman boasted. "I found this spot in my first month here. It's almost impossible to find window panels at ground level. All we get to see is sky, but here, best view of the lunar surface on the entire base if you ask me."

Carlo felt his breathing increase, his throat tighten as he gazed upon the vast landscape, unobstructed by buildings or power stations or hab facilities. Nothing but craters and white dust, settling eternally, stretching as far as he could see. And it called to him. Carlo stared at it, wide eyed, and felt it pulling him. And then he felt something else. An aching in his fingers. An itching on his scalp. And a tickle in his throat.

"Hey, you okay man?"

"Yeah," Carlo coughed, trying to hide the cold sweat on his brow behind the protective visor. "It's just overwhelming, you know. I should, I gotta-"

He stumbled backwards, away from the window, and the second he was out of sight of the clearly confused woman who had been so proud to show off her secret viewing location, he turned and sprinted for the greenhouse door.

Carlo couldn't sleep. He peered down at Lola, slumbering peacefully on his chest. He tried to keep his breathing steady so as not to disturb her. His anchor, his rock in this mad world. He knew he should tell her. But he had already put her through so much. He couldn't bring himself to do it. He gulped, and she sighed in her sleep, shifting just a little. Carlo winced, then returned to staring at the ceiling. It was probably just his imagination, his fear, his paranoia. No, it most certainly was. Probably.

"You've been quiet the last few days."

Carlo looked up from his dinner. Lola was watching him, studying him. While there was compassion in her smile, there was also a wariness in her eyes. A fear.

"I'm fine."

Lola kept examining him as he prodded at his food with a yet-otherwise-unused spoon.

"Why do you think we colonized the Moon?" Carlo asked after a few moments of silence.

"What? Are you, *you,* honestly asking me why we came here?"

"Humanity. We do you think we colonized the Moon? It's not a place we can survive naturally. It's not a place our ancestors visited since antiquity. But in countless cultures there are stories, imaginings of traveling to the Moon, living on its surface. Why? It's like we had an instinct to migrate, but what species has ever been compelled to go somewhere they've never been, where they can't even survive? Do you think…do you think there was something calling us here?"

"You think Neil Armstrong was one of you?"

Carlo didn't react, something Lola found incredibly disheartening. She usually knew how to lighten the mood with him.

"Carlo, what happened? Talk to me."

"It's nothing," he took her hand. "Nothing. Just tired, that's all."

Sleep did not come easy for Carlo over the next several nights. His eyes remained wide open, bloodshot, his pupils dancing back and forth as his mind sought distraction from something, something playing at the corners of his subconscious. Less than a whisper, but still impossible to ignore. A call. And every night, a little louder.

Carlo glanced down at Lola, still asleep. With steady, deliberate movements he lowered one foot from the bed. Then the other. The rest of his body followed, and he quietly grabbed his protective gear from the hook on the door as his limbs carried him into the hall. In total silence, Carlo crept through the colony of domes and tunnels, his focus unwaveringly fixated on a single objective. An image. A feeling.

He pulled the foliage to the side, despite the fact that he didn't even remember walking all the way to the greenhouse, on the other side of the colony from his hab. His pupils widened as his vision was filled with vast expanses of white dust. The last time he was here, the Moon, Sun, and Earth weren't in good positions relative to each other. The landscape was cast in shadow. But tonight, the light hit it perfectly, each grain of dust glistening white and pure, and a rich glow bathed the inside of the greenhouse. A sensation washed over Carlo, a need fulfilled, but in the back of his mind a new desire, a new need, taking shape. A whisper growing louder.

Carlo felt an aching in his fingers. He felt an itching on his scalp. He felt a tickle in his throat. He felt a hunger in his heart. With steady hands, Carlo removed his gloves. Then his jacket. His helmet.

He closed his eyes and took a slow breath, reveling in the sensation, face glowing in soft light. Then, his eyes shot open wide, his pupils dilating. There was a tickle in his throat. He coughed. The tickle returned, growing into a rumble. Then a growl. Then he opened his mouth, and howled.

"What are you doing back here? You're not supposed…WHAT THE-"

The officers exchanged puzzled looks. The man behind the glass, chained to the chair, hardly seemed the type.

"I heard the security guard looked like he'd been mauled by an animal."

"He's in bad shape, I know that much. Don't know how we would have found him if he hadn't been able to trigger the alarm, lockdown the greenhouse."

"How could something like that happen?"

"We'll have the security tapes soon. They should hold some answers."

The officers exchanged glances once more. One shrugged, and then pushed a button on the panel.

"Benandanti, you have a visitor," the officer's voice came over the intercom.

Lola burst into the holding room, throwing herself around Carlo and whispering frantically in his ear. The officers leaned into their monitors. All they could hear was Carlo collapsing into tears, shaking uncontrollably as he whispered in raspy, punctuated breaths:

"I'm sorry. I'm so sorry."

The officers looked at each other again.

"You can't be serious!" Lola's hands flew through the air, accentuating her outrage. "My husband suffered from lunar psychosis, from the stress of colonizing! I know the attack seems animalistic and it's a tragedy, but this has happened in other colonies. There are several documented cases of colonists-"

"-Mrs. Benandanti," the commander's tone was quiet. "We know what your husband is."

"Commander, do you hear yourself!? You're talking about…about fantasy! Mythology! This is absolute madness!"

"Call it whatever you like. It represents a real danger to this colony."

"This is-"

The commander held up a hand, and waved to his subordinate. Carlo was marched into the office, wrists and ankles bound in shackles, his head hanging low and his cheeks stained with tears.

"What is still unclear," the commander continued, "is how much you knew about this, Ma'am."

"Knew about what?" Lola breathed, exasperated, hands still over her head. The commander flicked a switch and on the monitor in the office a blurry image blinked to life. Amidst the grains and pixels, the movement of grey fur, a flashing of claws. On the audio, the scream of the guard, a howl. Carlo's head sunk lower. Lola turned white.

"So, did you know?" Asked the commander.

"Of course she didn't!" Carlo shouted suddenly, jumping to his feet. The guards pushed him back down, but he continued to struggle, spittle foaming at the edges of his mouth. "I never told her anything! I never told anyone!"

"Of course I knew!" Lola snapped, piercing Carlo with burning eyes, eyes which were then turned on the commander. "So when's the trial, *sir*?"

The commander sat, quiet. He sighed, and shook his head.

"I don't pretend to know what you are. I'd never believe it myself if not for these tapes. But if stories, rumors about you got out…this could end colonization as we know it. I'm sorry, but I have no choice."

He nodded to the guards and in an instant, Carlo and Lola were both seized, screaming as they were dragged from the room and thrown into the nearest airlock.

"I'll give you one minute." The commander's voice rang over the intercom. Carlo collapsed against Lola, sobbing.

"We should never have come here. I thought we could escape the curse by moving here, I thought- I'm sorry, Lo. I'm so sorry."

She hugged him, wrapping her arms around his still-chained body. They stood for a moment in silence.

"I never told you the other possibility I predicted," she said suddenly. Carlo sniffed, and looked up.

"What?"

"I told you I thought two outcomes were equally likely when we arrived. That living on the Moon would break the monthly curse, or…"

"That I'd…explode?"

"In a way. That being here would magnify it. I mean, stranger things, right? You knew the Moon was calling you. I thought maybe you'd become, I don't know, a superwolf."

"A…superwolf?"

"Yeah, you know, the mega alpha. King canine. Carlo, the wolf god."

Carlo couldn't help but crack a weak smile. Even here, even now, she was still trying to cheer him up.

"It's time. May God show you mercy."

The commander's voice echoed in the airlock and red lights began to flash. Lola squeezed Carlo tighter and he snarled at the door, a white-hot rage suddenly searing through his veins. It wasn't right. The injustice of it, for Lola to be here. He was a monster, he deserved this fate, but Lola, Lola was good, and kind, and innocent. It wasn't fair. He couldn't stand for it. He couldn't.

A tickle rose in Carlo's throat.

It grew quickly and rumbled in his chest. But as he bared his teeth, the airlock opened, ripping the war cry from his lungs.

And yet, this was not the only sensation Carlo was aware of in that moment. In that single, fleeting instant as the gates opened and he was sucked out, the airlock was flooded with light. Saturated with moonbeams.

He was first aware only of the fact that he was still aware. Aware of himself. Aware of his physical presence. And above all, aware of his rage.

Then, other experiences. He writhed as his fingers ached, nails stretching into claws. His snout elongated, teeth becoming fangs. His body itched, then exploded into fur, white, pristine, and cold as diamonds shimmering in the moonlight. He huffed, and sniffed, there was no air here to sniff and yet...he sniffed again, his senses attuning to the lunar surface. There she was. Lola's corpse, wreathed in a gossamer halo of still-settling dust. Carlo began to salivate, and licked his fangs. He could sense it. The blood frozen in her body. There was one oath he had made on Earth that he held sacred above all others. He had never broken it. Rage seared through his veins. He was about to.

There was a tickle in his throat.

"Commander, the security guard, he's awake."

The commander stood, surprised.

"We didn't think he'd make it."

"He's not going to, sir. He's barely clinging to life. But he's delirious, manic, screaming that he needs to go to the greenhouse. We're not sure why."

"We shall accommodate him," the commander nodded. The officer ran off to enforce the order, and the commander continued to puzzle over these new events. Why would the guard want to return to the scene of his attack? There was a spot nearby where many colonists liked to go and gaze upon the lunar surface. Perhaps the guard just wanted to see the Moon one last time. The guard would have his final request; the window panels had been sealed during the attack, but they were open again now. The greenhouse should be beautiful at this time of night, bathed in moonlight. At least the guard would expire in peace. It was unfortunate, the commander thought, but it was one less person to have to keep quiet about all of this.

The commander paced his office, mind working through the strangeness of the day. Something about the guard's request still bothered him. The commander paced, glancing out the small window in his office. He paced, then froze, and slowly traced his steps back to the window. He looked out again, squinting, then jumped as an alarm blared throughout the colony.

"What's going on?" He shouted down the hall.

"Alarm, from the greenhouse!"

"Report, now!"

"Commander, look!"

Throughout the colony, people froze in their tracks, their blood turning cold as, over the alarms, another sound pierced the chaos, an impossible sound, traveling through the vacuum of space outside the walls. A howl.

People pressed themselves against whatever windows they could find. All anyone could see were two massive shapes, glistening white in the moonlight, clouds of shimmering dust in their wakes, charging towards the dome.

A howl from outside. Another. And then a third, answering them, coming from the greenhouse.

Christopher Muscato is a writer and adjunct professor from the mountains of Colorado in the United States. He was the writer-in-residence for the High Plains Library District in 2017 and has published numerous short stories since then.

Ivanwolf

M.T. Johnson

Dawn cracked across the green blanket of tall pines that lay over the Rhodope mountains. A hazy gray mist crept along the forest floor, not to be confused with the steam rising from the werewolf's carcass below him. Its blue lifeless tongue spilled out from its maw, white foam bubbled over the jagged teeth, and its blank yellow eye, wide open, stared into the sky. Hot blood spilled over its abdomen into the frosted soil.

Fred, a Karelian Bear Dog, sniffed eagerly at the werewolf's corpse.

"You got a scent, lad?" Robert Hall said. Fred's wagging tail answered his question. He was a big dog, wolf-like, with a thick black coat that turned to a creamy white on his belly and legs. A Finnish breed, bred in the old days for hunting bears—strong, fearless and aggressive, handy when living in the Bulgarian wilderness where such animals lurked.

Fred sniffed the werewolf's body again and zigzagged up the hill, his nose rarely leaving the ground. Robert slung his Baikal MP-153 shotgun over his shoulder and jogged up the hill, gripping onto the pines as he did to avoid slipping when it got steep.

His breath escaped him in steamy plumes by the time he got to the top. Fred was already halfway down the bank, following the trail. Robert leaned against a tree and took a deep breath. *Not the man you used to be, Rob,* he thought, tired.

Hunting was a hobby that had kept him fit in his early retirement, but age had slowed him. Back in the military, his Corporal would have had him doing one hundred press-ups if he caught Robert panting from running up a hill. *Give yourself a break, big man. We've been hunting before the sun rose.*

Robert wanted to get a head start on the werewolves, coming out just before dawn to catch them in the woods as they underwent their metamorphosis, and indeed he had. The beast back at the bottom of the hill was hit with a shot to the chest, and a second to the stomach. The dawn had already begun its work on the werewolf. It was smaller and slower, its senses dulled; it didn't even notice Fred's scent before Robert was in shooting range.

He started down the hill, trying to go fast but still minding his step. Fred looked up at him from the bottom of the bank and barked. It echoed through the snowy forest.

"You telling me to hurry up or trying to warn me?" Robert yelled and looked around, scratching his grizzly brown beard, peppered with gray. Fred cocked his head and barked at him again.

"I'm coming, I'm coming. Cheeky bugger." He laughed.

Robert followed Fred as he continued following the scent that would lead them to the werewolf den. He hoped to kill their new alpha along with the rest of his pack while they slept, or at least while they were weak. *What's he going to look like this time?* He thought. The last alpha he killed was twice the size of the werewolves in its pack, and it was albino—snow-white fur with blood-red eyes. Claws like daggers and muscles like it shot more steroids than a hulking bodybuilder.

Baba Svetla, an old Bulgarian woman from the small village of Malka (thirty-minute drive down the road from Robert's lakeside house), was grateful for his help with their werewolf infestation last time round. That was five years ago, the first time Robert had fought the beasts. His hunting abilities proved to be a good transferable skill. He hoped that would be the last of them, but now Malka village had a second pest problem. Only this time they seemed more… *organized*. It started with people's livestock being stolen in the night; first thought to be the work of thieves, only to have the hounds track the animals deep into the woods or some ominous dark cavern with a mangled carcass at the end of the trail. Not long after the livestock, people started going missing; faster than before. There were rarely corpses at the end of those trails. The scent would be lost, and the attacks became more frequent.

Robert wondered how many local villagers he'd had to kill in his time hunting werewolves. Alexander Grubov, the owner of Pletivo, a local general goods shop, went missing two weeks ago; could he have been one of the casualties? Maybe he was the one Robert just shot earlier. He lowered his head and sighed. *I liked Alex.*

Snow crunched under his boots as they climbed further into the hills. Robert stayed alert for any sound, not planning to be caught by a bear, wolf, or their wolf-man kin this far from home. Birds flapped from the trees above, and twigs snapped beneath his step. Every sudden sound sent a jolt through his veins.

Fred led him to a hill larger than any they had yet to climb. His muzzle lit up at whatever scent was on the trees here; Robert felt like he could smell it too. A dank smell like an old carpet, like dogs.

Wolves.

Aye, we're near. Robert took his semi-automatic shotgun from his shoulder and loaded another shell. His fingers twitched and his hand shook. He felt scared because they had walked for miles and only found one werewolf. The others must have run back to their filthy dens before Robert came out.

"Getting smarter, are we?" He mumbled to himself, trying to sound brave, but his mouth went dry. The thought of how many werewolves there might be in one of their dens, weak or not, made his blood curdle. Picking them off one by one was easy—when they're all together…

For a moment he thought of fleeing and trying again a different night. He slapped himself. *You made a promise to Baba Svetla to cull them. For her daughter, and everyone else they took.* If he left now, how many people would go missing the next night? How much would the pack swell? He couldn't afford to wait.

You and Fred against a whole pack? Another voice from his subconscious protested.

Get a grip! Werewolves during the day? Scrawny little ferrets they are. One shot of the Baikal will scatter them like crows!

Fred pressed uphill and Robert followed. He decided to cull them all today. The dog led him past great twisted oak, a rocky cave opening next to it. The smell of dog, death, and urine reeked now. Fred dashed around the entrance, waiting for Robert. Patches of dry blood made a twisted trail into the cave. Robert took a deep breath and turned the flashlight on the side of the shotgun on.

"Stay close, Freddy boy." He beckoned the dog to his side. Fred's ears pricked up and he snarled a little, sensing whatever lurked inside the dark cave. They entered.

Their footsteps echoed through the rocky cave. Bloodstains, new and old, decorated the walls. Fred sniffed around and tried to dart into the cave, but Robert didn't let him.

The rotten, sweetish odor of death hung heavy here. He stepped forward carefully, pointing the shotgun in every dark corner to make sure it was clear. The light behind them was a small dot now. Robert looked back one more time before stepping further into the cave.

The light behind them slowly faded; Robert felt trapped. Eyes wide and hands clutching the shotgun with a solid grip like it was an extension of his body.

Sounds like rocks falling clapped through the pitch-black ahead. Robert froze and pointed the shotgun into the void. Fred snarled and proceeded.

"I'll trust your senses from here on, boy," Robert whispered and followed the hound.

They walked for a few minutes, the light of the entrance long behind them, before Fred stopped and barked into the darkness. Robert brought the butt of the shotgun firmly to his shoulder and pointed ahead, waiting.

It leaped from the darkness with a velocity that somehow took Robert by surprise. His mind's description of the daytime werewolves earlier: *scrawny little ferrets*, was fairly accurate, but that didn't make them any less terrifying. The thing that jumped from the dark was not quite a werewolf, but not a man either. It sat in-between, like a skinny feral human. Its eyes were that of a canine: wide and amber. Long thin hair covered its pale flesh, its claws reached out, and foam fizzed from behind its sharp teeth.

Before Robert could react, Fred latched onto its arm and ragged, sending it tumbling to the floor. Its screech was like a knife to the ear. Blood squirted from its arm as Fred yanked. It clawed and bit at Fred, trying to free itself, but Robert was already above it by then and brought the butt of the shotgun down on its skull like a hammer. The first blow sent it unconscious with a whimper. The next five killed it.

Robert pointed the gun ahead, illuminating the way to make sure it was clear. If it had friends nearby, they definitely heard that. Fresh blood glistened over Fred's mouth and ran down his paws. Robert quickly checked him for any wounds. None. They pressed forward.

The cave got narrow at some points, not even big enough for him and Fred to go through side by side. The rocky walls dug into his hips when he had to squeeze through, and the ceiling was lined with sharp rocks like icicles.

Why aren't there more? was a question that kept repeating itself in his head. The more he asked, the more anxious he got. The entrance of the cave reeked of them, even Robert could tell that, yet since they set out, they had only seen two werewolves. *Maybe there weren't as many as I thought? No. That can't be. They've been ravaging the livestock and harassing Malka village for days.*

Robert pushed through a narrow opening into a wider cavern. By the sound of his footsteps, he could tell the cavern was massive, like an underground cathedral. His light didn't touch the ceiling. Fred followed through and snarled. He barked into the darkness.

"*Shhhh!*" He nudged Fred with his foot. God knew how many werewolves could be in here when his flashlight didn't light up the whole room.

Two small silver orbs seemed to float amidst the darkness. Robert jumped and shone the light on them. The orbs were two silver eyes, like a little pair of full moons, attached to a jet-black wolf. A streak of gray fur raced up its nose and past the eyes. The wolf was beautiful, yet it carried a ghastly aura about it. What was it doing here?

Fred squared up and barked at it, trying to attack before Robert grabbed him. "We're not here for wolves, Fred. Get back."

The black wolf got closer and Robert pointed the shotgun at it. "That's about far enough, lad. I have no quarrel with you." He thrust the gun like a spear, trying to scare the wolf off. It only stared at him.

Move out the way, you stupid thing. I don't want to kill you.

Fred barked at it again. The wolf took no notice. It was twice the size of Fred, but Fred was bred to kill bears. The two of them could handle the strange wolf no problem. The wolf raised its head and howled — the sound chilled Robert to the bone. It was so unnatural, *unholy*.

He kept his shotgun trained on it, both wanting and not wanting to shoot. He wanted to stop that paranormal noise coming from the wolf's mouth, but was that worth wasting a shot? Robert had half a mind to let Fred at it.

Footsteps got louder behind the wolf. Many footsteps.

"Right," Robert croaked. "Fred, get close." He beckoned Fred between his legs with his free hand while keeping his shotgun on the wolf. One of the werewolves, scrawny and hunched in its half-human form, walked in front of the black wolf. Robert pointed the shotgun at the werewolf. Slowly more and more wolf-men materialized from the blackness behind and stood in front of the wolf.

Fred snarled from beneath Robert but didn't dare to run forward. He was trained well to stay in this defensive position. Robert slowly edged backward, not taking the gun and light away from the pack of scrawny werewolves and the black wolf, now slowly fading behind the increasing number of its wolf-men defenders.

The loud grumbles of the werewolves made his hairs stand. He wanted to shoot the wolf he presumed was the pack leader, strange as it was, but feared it would send the twenty-plus wolf-men into a frenzied charge while he was still in open space. Robert backed into the narrow opening where he came from, the scrawny werewolves slowly pressed forward, cautious. He didn't want to startle them… yet.

Fred slipped through first, and Robert backed into it. When he felt the narrow rocky wall brushing his back, he pressed his shotgun against his shoulder and fired into the werewolf pack.

The thundering boom of the shot cracked like a cannon and rang through the cavern. The flare lit their faces in a white flash, followed by a gout of blood exploding from the neck of a wolf-man. The rest of them screamed and charged. Robert fired two more, sending one of the werewolves tumbling down; a few more tripped over it.

"WITH ME, FRED!" He bellowed and ran through the dark narrow cave as fast as he could. Fred slipped past his legs and ran forward. Robert tried to reload the shotgun while running but his arms kept hitting the wall. He dropped a shell.

"Dammit!" He barked and tried another—it clumsily slid into the chamber as he ran.

He heard them shuffling and huffing behind him, their nails clawing against the rock.

A small light appeared in the distance and got larger as they ran. Robert's heart leaped. *The exit!* His excitement dulled when he noticed the cave getting wider, meaning more of them could follow him through. Their sharp screeches got louder. Robert burst into a sprint, losing all feeling in his legs, adrenaline pumping through him.

For a brief moment, he felt like a soldier again. Feeling this exhausted was a common occurrence. They did runs that made this look tame. He saw himself running through an obstacle course, wet muddy grass surrounded by ropes, water, and wooden posts, then Nigeria, then the deserts of Iraq, scorching hot surrounded by hostiles. *Always running, always fighting… always hunting.*

The exit was so close he could taste the fresh air. Fred got out first. Robert had a foot out before a sharp claw yanked his fur-lined leather coat. He lost his balance and fell out of the cave, rolling down the bank with a halfling werewolf latched onto his back.

Fred barked and charged the werewolf trying to ravage Robert, knocking it over and going for its throat.

It growled and scratched at Fred. Robert tried to help the dog but saw five more of them running down the bank.

"Two seconds, boy!" He yelled, aimed, and fired at the charging wolf-men. He shot one in the leg. It cried in pain and fell over, rolling down the bank and leaving a trail of blood in its wake. The next shot went straight through the chest of another, a spurt of blood exploded from its heart.

The other halfling werewolves fled back into the cave. And thank God, too. His shotgun clicked when he pulled the trigger on the fleeing wolf-men—empty.

Fred and the werewolf he had pulled off Robert still scrambled on the floor behind him. Both of them were covered in blood, growling and biting at each other. Robert ran to them and kicked the wolf-man over. It whimpered and tried to flee, but Fred didn't give him an inch. Fred threw himself against the werewolf and clamped his jaw around its throat.

The werewolf slowly stopped struggling; its screams became muffled gurgles as it choked on its own blood.

When the werewolf died, Fred came limping back to him. He whimpered, not unlike the wolf-men moments ago.

"What's happened to you, Freddy?" Robert knelt by him, checking the area for more werewolves, it was clear. He brushed Fred's soft fur where it was red and glistening, revealing the skin beneath. He spotted multiple scratches around Fred's legs and back, none deep enough to look concerning. Most of the blood staining his fur must have belonged to the wolf-men.

Fred whimpered again.

"Stop being a baby. Just a few scratches, that's all." Robert chuckled, relieved the struggle was over. He tried to put the thought of having to go back in the werewolf den out of his mind for now. Maybe he'd come back with some help next time, or with more weapons. He underestimated the halfling werewolves and didn't expect to see *that* many.

Warm blood trickled over his fingers when he brushed some fur over the top of Fred's front leg. A small circle of teeth marks oozed blood. Robert grunted and scratched Fred's head. "We'll get that fixed up for you, boy. Just need to make it back to ours first. Come on."

He pulled up outside Ivana Banova's house in Malka village. She was a veterinarian who retired early and came to live deep in the country with her husband. Robert stepped out of his old Range Rover with Fred and opened the big metal gate to her house. The old metal screeched as he pulled it.

The house was big by rural village standards, with a balcony and a basement. The front area was spacious with a cobbled path leading to the vegetable patches around the back. Her guard dog, a massive German Shepherd named Bobby, ran onto the balcony and barked loudly at them. Fred barked back and Robert told him to shut up.

Ivana walked out the front door and lit a cigarette. "Hello, Robert," she said in Bulgarian, which sounded like, *"Zdravey, Robert."*

"Hello," he replied, also in Bulgarian, hearing his thick English accent.

Her eyes fell to Fred limping by his side, and she figured out the reason for his visit. Despite being in her late thirties, Ivana didn't look a day over twenty-five. She had smooth olive skin and sea-green eyes. Her shiny black hair was tied in a ponytail that swung past her lower back.

Robert explained their journey to the werewolf den and his analysis of Fred's injuries. Ivana took him to the spare room that she used as a vet room for the local animals since there wasn't another vet for miles. Robert lifted Fred onto the table and Ivana examined him, brushing his fur out of the way and cleaning it with a damp cloth. Blotches of red stained it.

"How's Stefan? I didn't see him today," Robert asked.

"He went to Sofia yesterday on business. Staying for a week," Ivana said.

"He left now? With the werewolves around?"

Fred flinched when Ivana looked over the bite wound. "It should be alright. I have Bobby and Angel to protect me. Stefan left a gun for me, and I have needles full of powerful anesthetic in case one of the beasts happens to get through everything else."

"I ought to take some with me next time I go hunting them," Robert laughed and scratched his back where the werewolf clawed him. It left an irritating itch.

"I can't believe you just took Fred when you went. Especially with all the people they've been attacking. Surely there's dozens of them?"

"Thought I'd catch a few more before I found their little nest," Robert stroked Fred's back. "I was wrong about that."

"You should have asked Stanil or Ogi to come with you. They've been hunting too." She patted Fred on the head. "Then this visit wouldn't be necessary, hm?"

"As I said, I didn't expect to see so many. Is the bite bad? The scratches seem to have healed on the way. But I was worried the bite might be infected…" *Next thing I know Fred will become a werewolf too,* he thought jokingly.

"It's not as bad as it looks. I suppose you're lucky the dog was bitten in the daytime when werewolves are weak. Otherwise, he might have been short a leg." She went to her cabinet and rummaged through various bottles and boxes. "Cleaning it is relatively simple. I just need to stop the little amount of bleeding, shave the area, flush the wound, then disinfect it."

Ivana laid a few small bottles on the table, opened one of them, a blood-clotting mineral powder, and sprinkled it over the bite wound. When the bleeding stopped, she shaved the area, struggling to hold Fred still. Robert told him to sit and stay put. She applied a pressurized saline wound wash to flush out any bacteria and debris and then disinfected it with a diluted Povidone iodine solution. "All done," she said and gave Fred a treat.

His eyes lit up and he nabbed it. In his mind's eye, Robert saw Fred as a puppy again, laying on the vet's table for his vaccinations. A small bundle of black and white fur and two moony brown eyes, crying at the vet trying to stick a needle into him. Robert remembered yelling at him to sit still, but the pup wouldn't listen. It took a long time to drill some discipline into him. Hours spent using treats and making the puppy follow his hands while he spoke the commands: "Sit," "stay," "roll over," and so on. Fred's playful nature in his youth gave Robert a few laughs; always trying to nip him or pinch treats. Play fighting him got harder the more he grew up, but never duller. Fred's bites got worse, and he got strong enough to knock Robert over when he wanted. A memory of them tumbling through the mud on a soaking day after Fred had spotted a squirrel and went for it while the leash twisted around Robert's legs and tripped him over popped into his head. Robert smirked, he loved that little bugger.

"Thank you, Ivana," Robert smiled.

"I can order you the supplies for minor wounds if you'd like. Then you can do it yourself, wounds like that don't require veterinary attention if you have the right stuff." Ivana put her things back in the cabinet. Fred jumped off the table, a bald spot on his front leg.

"I like to see the experts," Robert chuckled. "But I will buy some if you order them."

They walked through to the living room. A fire burned in a metal fireplace at the center of the room. Logs cracked and shot embers up the chimney pipe. A large bowl half-full of Shopska salad sat on the dining table. Ivana offered him some, but he politely refused.

"I was wondering, Ivana…" He scratched his beard. "Should the werewolf bite on Fred be concerning? Do they, you know, turn?"

Ivana's eyes rolled up and she hummed, wondering. "I don't think so. Humans turn over the course of twenty-four hours, and I've never seen an animal affected by the condition; come to think of it, I've never even known them to attack canines. Has he not been bitten before?"

"No. This is only the second werewolf infestation I've seen while I've lived here and after each encounter, Fred came away with little injuries, scratches at most. You see, Fred normally goes for the arms and legs, and I'm always close by to finish the wolf-men off; he's never had to fight one alone until today. He got caught this time because he pulled the beast off my back and scrambled with it." Robert scratched his head, oddly, the question of werewolf bites affecting other animals never crossed his mind until now; he always assumed the affliction was exclusive to humans. *Maybe I'm just paranoid.* "These werewolves seemed… *different* from the others. The pack was a bit cleverer, bigger, and their alpha was a big black wolf." Robert looked at Fred, who was innocently wagging his tail, with worry.

"The wolf's presence among them is strange… but I'm sure Fred will be fine." She knelt and stroked Fred. "Won't you? You're a strong boy, aren't you?"

"You're the expert," Robert let out a weak laugh and looked back down at the small teeth marks on Fred's bald spot. *The vet said it's nothing to worry about. That should be the end of it, right?* Robert replayed her words again and again in his head, but that didn't calm him. He kept imagining Fred becoming one of those grotesque humanoid ferrets during the day and a killing machine by night. Thinking about Fred standing on his hind legs trying to murder his owner in the night sent a chill up Robert's spine. Spending years working in the military and as a private military contractor had taught him to expect the worst at all times. Expect to be shot at, expect the enemies to be all around you, and expect to fight for your goddamn life. His retirement hadn't stopped him from picturing foes around every corner.

"Did you need anything else?" Ivana said.

"No, that was all. Thank you again, Ivana. We should be on our way now." Robert beckoned Fred to come with him.

"My pleasure," she said. "Do come back if I can help again. We all need it in times like these. But we will pull through together, as the village always has."

Robert drove home with Fred in the passenger seat across the bumpy dirt road. Sleep didn't come easy that night. For hours he rolled around in the sheets. The wind howled outside the window. After getting up and downing a shot of rakia, he buried his head in the pillow. He went to sleep thinking of the bite on Fred's leg.

A thick iron-rimmed oaken door opened before him. It led into a stone corridor lined with torches. Robert walked into the castle. The fiery warmth of the torches licked his face. A small clattering came from down the hall, a gray wolf.

Robert froze, trying to reach for his shotgun, axe, or combat knife. To his terror, they weren't there. *Why am I wandering around without my kit?*

The wolf turned around and walked to a door, which opened when the wolf tapped against it. It got up and made to walk in, looking at him. When it noticed that he wasn't following, it stopped and sat by the open door.

Robert squinted. *Is it… waiting for me?*

He stepped forward, looking around for more wolves. The gray wolf lurched up with excitement and made for the door again, making sure Robert followed. He took another step, and another, slowly getting more comfortable. The wolf's tail wagged, and his legs twitched, desperate to walk through. Robert decided it was safe and followed.

The door led to a great hall; its floor and walls were gleamy obsidian. Finely carved columns shot up at the sides of the enormous dark room and arched over in Gothic patterns. A roaring fire baked the room from a huge hearth, spraying embers like dragon breath. The strangest thing in the room was the big dining table in the middle. A man sat at the head, and his guests appeared to be a pack of wolves, all with their own seats at the table.

The gray wolf led him to an empty seat on the table. Robert sat. The man at the head raised his eyes and smiled; he looked oddly familiar. His long hair was jet-black with a gray streak running down the side; it fell over his piercing silver eyes. He wore a fur-lined black overcoat that exposed his hairy chest. He wrapped the curly tip of his mustache on his finger and said, "Hungry, Robert?"

Knives and forks clattered around him, and he realized the wolves at the table dug into slabs of raw meat using fine silverware. *Why the hell are the wolves using knives and forks?*

"Who are you?" Robert said.

"My name is Ivan. But my friends here call me Ivanwolf." Ivan cut into his raw steak, dripping blood when he sliced through with his silver knife and ate. "You can call me either. I don't mind."

The gray wolf that led him into the hall appeared at his side, holding a tray in its mouth. On the tray was a plate holding a sloppily cut steak, red and raw, blood dripping down the sides of the plate. Robert didn't take it.

"What's the matter? That's venison. Delicious, if I may say so." Ivan said, chewing his food as red fluid dripped down his mouth.

"I don't eat raw meat. You ever heard of food poisoning, man?" Robert snapped, still glancing at the wolves using knives and forks. *Why the hell are they doing that?*

His brow curled. "I'm not familiar with it, no. However, I would be a terrible host to not accommodate your needs." Ivan's ghastly silver eyes fell on the wolf holding the tray. After a moment, it went by the hearth and set the tray down near it.

Ivan didn't speak until the meat was brought back, brown and steaming. Robert reluctantly took it. Without seasoning, it smelt bland.

"I suppose you're wondering why you're here, Robert?" Ivan asked.

Robert cut a slice of venison, juicy and pink in the middle, and ate. It tasted as it smelt. "Enlighten me."

"You owe me some compensation, Robert." Ivan stared at him. Robert stopped eating.

"Compensation?" He scoffed. "For what?"

"You spilled the blood of my kin in my own home. You owe me." The wolves at the table barked like a cheering crowd.

"That's impossible. I've never been here, I don't know who you are, and I haven't killed any wolves."

Ivan smiled. "Appearances can be deceiving. You looked me right in the eye before you shot my kin."

Robert glanced anxiously at the wolves clattering away with their cutlery, clutching his knife. "I shot the vile creatures who terrorized Malka village, *werewolves*, not wolves. The only strange thing in their den was a black wolf, not you—"

Appearances can be deceiving.

Fear clogged his throat. *Is Ivan... the wolf? Ivanwolf...* Surely this was a paranoid thought, a figment of his terror.

"Finally caught on, have you?" Ivan laughed, and the wolves howled in unison. "You may have realized I'm not your ordinary *werewolf,* as you would call it."

"What are you then?"

"A wolf," he grinned.

"I'm not going to play games with you," Robert warned, slicing his venison in half.

Ivan slammed his fist, the table shook. "Nor am I." The wolves stopped and looked at him with cocked heads. "You'll hear my offer, or you're going to die."

"Hah! I'll kill all your pups with this knife and fork. Try me!" Robert felt a surge of strength rise in him, ready to fight them all to the death like a cornered animal.

Ivan laughed again, and the wolves cackled with him. A horrid sound if Robert ever heard one. "You may not be as ready for that as you think... Your death will be arranged by other means should you refuse my offer."

Robert squinted, not sure what to make of that statement. "What's this offer, then?"

"It's quite simple," Ivan took another bite. "First, you never kill another one of my *werewolves* again. Second, you will kill the others who hunt my kin. Quite simple, really."

"Are you mad? If I kill men of the village, I'm as good as dead anyway," Robert spat. Even if he could get away with killing the other hunters, the werewolves would keep prowling around Malka village, taking livestock, and kidnapping others. All of that blood would be on his hands. *I'd sooner die.*

"Then I'll have you killed, Robert," Ivan said sternly.

Robert laughed. "How? I've been killing werewolves for years." He looked around at the wolves using their cutlery, *werewolves*, he thought. "They're not very bright."

"My agent is no ordinary wolf-man. In fact, he lives in your home," Ivan smiled.

Icy tendrils gripped Robert's heart, and he remembered the bite on Fred's leg. Surely he didn't mean Fred? "You're bluffing," Robert croaked. "Dogs can't turn. My vet said so."

The wolves laughed again. Robert tried for another bite of venison, but his hands shook.

"Are you sure about that?" Ivan said, brow raised above those hideous silver wolf's eyes.

No. He wasn't sure about that at all. That question was on his mind constantly, and the ghastly wolf-man-thing called Ivan confirmed it for him. He seemed to be a greater authority on the subject than a vet. But *a vet would know, right? It's their job to know these things, isn't it? After all, werewolves are animals too...*

"Yes, I'm sure," Robert said, almost a whisper.

Ivan cackled and leaned back in his chair, twirling his mustache. "Oh, Robert. Your eyes tell a different story." He stood up and raised his arm to silence the wolves at the table. "I will ask one more time. Do you accept my terms?"

Robert wondered if Ivan was bluffing about Fred. Would he really choose his security in exchange for the lives of the villagers he came to know in his retirement? Even if it meant losing Fred... having to kill him? Surely this can't be real; it must be a dream of some sort. The wolves using cutlery, the strange wolfman at the head of their pack. *Werewolves.*

"You're sweating, Robert," Ivan said calmly. "I hope you're considering taking my offer."

Robert pictured Fred as a puppy again. He pictured Malka village and the folk who lived there. Baba Nusha picking her tomatoes and selling them at a stall, donkeys pulling people on carriages, the smell of livestock, and the baking sun in the summertime. All their lives at stake…

"Take your offer and go to hell," Robert spat. He got up from the table and walked to the door, trying to force himself out of this dream.

"Your dog's mine now, Robert!" Ivan wailed from the table, his voice ringing through the great hall. "He'll kill you! I promise you he will!"

The vet said Fred would be fine. Ivana wouldn't mislead me. She could be wrong.

Robert stepped out of the castle and stood at a drawbridge. Two full moons lit the night sky in a lunar glow. He looked up at them. They looked like a pair of eyes. Angry eyes, *hungry eyes.*

Robert lurched from his pillow, drenched in cold sweat. "Oh my God, I knew that was a dream." *An oddly specific dream.* A dream he could recall in great detail. Some dreams felt like that, though. Once he had a dream where he had to kill dozens of velociraptors with a samurai sword, that one felt real. And another where he had to fight his father. Still… this wolf dream felt very *real.* He rubbed his head and got out of bed. A cold breeze covered him in goose pimples.

His heart froze when he looked out of the window. A full moon, shiny and silver. Robert nearly screamed when he saw the other, and then laughed when he realized it was the moon's reflection in Beglik lake. The lake looked black and still in the night. Tranquil.

"Just a dream."

A ghastly howl rang dimly in the distance. He recognized the paranormal sound instantly, the black wolf. *Ivanwolf.*

Maybe I'll stay up for the night and keep an eye on the windows. Robert put on some jeans and a thick jumper, and he took his combat knife out from under the bed and slung it at his side.

He noticed Fred's dog bed in the corner of the room was empty. A lump caught in his throat; Fred never wandered in the night. "Freddy?" Robert called. No answer.

Of all the times you could be awake at night-time, you just had to pick this goddamn night, didn't you, Freddy? Oh, this must be some kind of joke. The dream wasn't real it wasn't real!

"Freddy?" He tried again. Muffled scratches came from downstairs, like scraping wood with a knife.

Robert stepped carefully down the stairs, clutching his knife, wincing every time the wood creaked. *Why are you being quiet, it's just Fred for God's sake!*

Is it, though? A voice in the back of his mind replied.

Robert switched the lights on downstairs. He slowly walked into the kitchen; the scratching got louder. Fred was clawing at the door that led into the garage. *The meat room.* Robert was using the garage to store wild game meat from their previous hunts. The winter months acted as a refrigerator.

"What you doing, Freddy?" Robert said. The dog looked at him, his eyes wide with hunger and drool oozed from his maw.

"You've got food in your bowl, boy." Robert pointed at the bowl, half-full of dog food. Fred barked and clawed at the door, chipping it away in small flakes.

Fred's strange behavior made him anxious. Robert walked to the fridge and took out a large rump steak he was saving for tomorrow, inwardly hoping it would calm Fred down.

"Here you go, you big baby." He threw the steak, and it slapped against the floor. Fred lunged at it with a hunger Robert had never seen in him before. He ate the steak in three big gulps and dashed to the fridge for more.

"Hey!" Robert snapped. "You've had enough!"

Fred barked and cried and paced around the kitchen. Robert saw the bite on Fred's front leg and his eyes bulged with fear. The teeth marks had become glossy and black, with thin black veins expanding into Fred's skin. The infection grew as Robert watched.

"Oh, Freddy," Robert sighed. "I think Ivana was wrong about you."

"He's mine now," Ivan, *the black wolf,* had said in his dream, a dream that Robert now thought was something more than a dream. Tears swelled in Robert's eyes as he gripped his knife, trying not to think about what he might have to do. Was Fred going to transform? Would he get so hungry that he would try to eat Robert?

Maybe I can drive him to Ivana's after he's been fed. I'm sure she'll appreciate me rushing into her house at three in the morning. I can't kill him based on a dream, no matter how real it seemed. But he was thinking about it. A slave to the fear in his heart.

What if Ivana suggested putting Fred down? The constant thought of his beloved dog's death loomed in his mind. In an act of sympathy, Robert took the garage key from the counter and unlocked the door. Fred jumped and tried to race in, but Robert grabbed him by the collar. "Wait, boy. Sit!" He thought that with the chance of Fred dying, he might as well give him a nice feast, just in case. That, and he was worried about how erratic Fred's behavior could become if he didn't get any food. One of the hanging deer carcasses would keep him busy for a while.

Fred barked and jerked forward, pulling Robert with him.

"STOP!" Robert boomed. Fred lunged and tried to bite him; his jaw snapped at thin air.

Robert jumped in shock and let go. Fred ran to one of the skinned hanging deer and dug his teeth into it, ragging and tugging. The chain holding it rattled and the meat tore.

Robert became scared. Not of Fred. He was never scared of Fred, but he had the eerie feeling this was not Fred anymore. Fred hadn't dared to bite him in aggression since he was a pup, and he always obeyed commands. The dog's behavior wasn't the only thing creeping Robert out, it was the dog's size. Fred looked a little bit bigger, or was it in his head?

Oh Jesus he could be turning. If Fred was turning, Robert thought he would have a few hours to take him to Ivana's and have her check him before he jumped to any conclusions; based on how long humans turned.

But he's not a human.

Even now a part of Robert didn't want to believe anything was wrong, determined that his dream was nothing more than that, that Ivan or Ivanwolf was a figment of his imagination, a personification of his paranoia.

Robert slowly walked back towards Fred. The dog was too busy munching into the carcass that both of them had hunted. He put a hand on Fred's back and stroked slowly, clutching his knife in the other hand. Fred didn't respond.

A tear dripped from his eye. *It's not over yet. Stop worrying. Get ready and take him to Ivana's while he's eating.*

Sensing that Fred cared more about eating than what Robert was doing, Robert knelt by the dog, stroking his back. He carefully leaned in closer, hugging Fred as a million terrible scenarios of Fred's death or change raced through his mind. He needed this moment.

"I'm sorry I let that werewolf bite you. But you were just protecting me, weren't you boy?" Robert buried his head in Fred's soft black fur, stroking his back and crying. "You've always been protecting me here. You've always been a good lad."

Fred snapped and chewed the raw meat. Memories came back to him. Memories of when he first saw Fred at the breeder's establishment, beady eyes, and a little tongue hanging from his mouth as he panted. He remembered the two of them sitting on a hill after their first hunting trip. Robert had just shot a squirrel with an arrow, and Fred retrieved it like they were playing fetch. Robert then skinned and gutted the squirrel, and spit-roasted it over a fire as they sat and watched the dim sun falling behind a hill amidst the magnificent violet sky. They had shared supper that evening.

Robert got up in tears and went to the bedroom for his shotgun and car keys. The shotgun was a precaution; better to have it in case Fred's condition… worsened. On the way out he noticed Fred's shoulder blades looked sharper, the snapping of his jaw louder. Robert wondered if he would be too big to get out of the car by the time he got to Ivana's.

He got the shotgun from his cabinet and dug around for a box of shells. The first was empty, so he opened the second and loaded five into the shotgun. After getting his car keys he went back downstairs.

This was when Robert realized they wouldn't be going to Ivana's. Fred was standing on his hind legs, using his front legs to hold himself up against the deer. His front paws now looked more like *fingers*, fingers with sharp claws, slowly elongating by the second. His shoulders were broader, and his ears had grown. Fred turned around and looked at Robert, his eyes glowed yellow. Fred's eyes fell on the shotgun.

"Fred…" Robert gasped and tried to raise his shotgun, but his right arm felt limp and his hands shook.

Fred snarled at him and barked. A deep thunderous boom. It sent a shock through Robert that shook his bones and paused his heart. Fred dashed through the door, baring his teeth.

Robert's arm seemed to act of its own accord and swung the shotgun up, his finger squeezing the trigger. He shot too low, hitting the kitchen island. The corner of the marble top exploded and sent tiny pebbles across the room.

Fred, now a growing werewolf, was on top of him. Robert pressed the shotgun up against his dog's throat like a barbell. *God, he's gotten heavy.* Robert pushed up with all his strength, keeping that drooling maw inches from his face. Fred's breath was steamy and smelt like stale meat and blood.

Robert etched his thumb towards the trigger. It was a crazy idea and could cost him his life if it backfired, but he couldn't think of another way to get this enormous, and growing, beast off him. He squeezed the trigger with his thumb. A bright flare flashed to the left of his face, blinding him for a split second, and the loud crack of the shot left a high-pitched ringing in his ear. The gun flew to the right out of his hand and hit the side of the kitchen island; the shot had sent an explosion of wooden chips from the drawer.

Fred roared and fell back, dazed. The leather strap of the shotgun clung to Fred's newly grown claw and fell out of Robert's reach as the werewolf recoiled.

Robert scurried off the floor and bolted out of the kitchen. He wanted to go out of the front door, past the living room, then remembered the damn keys were in the kitchen. He ran upstairs. *I can jump out of my bedroom window and make it to the car. Drive to Malka village and get some help.* The fall would hurt, but better that than being torn to shreds. Maybe he could check the kitchen to see if Fred left so he could retrieve his shotgun, *maybe.*

He blitzed into his bedroom and slammed the door, taking the chair from his desk and wedging it between the door handle and the floor. Heavy footsteps crept up the hall, the wood screeching closer and closer. Robert put his slippers and coat on and then opened the window; freezing wind washed over his sweaty face. The door behind him thudded, then the wood cracked. Robert turned. Three nails like spear-tips stuck through the door.

Robert looked out of the window, and he froze. The drop didn't seem so big in his head. Wood crunched behind him. His heart threw itself against his ribcage; he climbed onto the windowsill. The wind howled, and his skin broke out in gooseflesh.

The door shattered open behind him and he saw those feral yellow eyes. Robert jumped. His insides turned to liquid and he crashed into a hedge, rolling over onto the cold wet grass. Pain stabbed through his shoulder and ribs. The window shattered above him, and the creature that shot through it was bigger than any werewolf Robert had ever seen, far more beast than man.

That split second where Fred, completely metamorphosed, crashed through the window and eclipsed the sky above him was etched into his memory forever. His furry belly was covered in creamy white fur, like the fur on his arms and legs; a pitch-black coat covered the rest of him. Muscles bulged under the fur. He was barrel-chested with broad shoulders and arms like logs. Fred crashed further away than Robert and rolled down a small bank toward Lake Beglik.

Robert got up and sprinted for the car. Fred barked in the distance, and already Robert heard the barks getting louder. He ran round to the front of the house and clicked the unlock button on the car keys. The Range Rover's indicator lights flashed yellow.

He opened the door, jumped in the driver's seat, and slammed it shut behind him. He stuck his key in the ignition and twisted. The front lights came on, and the engine clicked rapidly, refusing to start.

Fred appeared from the darkness in front of the headlights and charged, running on all fours like a gorilla. The engine kept clicking. "Come on, you bastard! Start!"

Robert boomed. The engine roared to life; Robert stuck it in drive and slammed the pedal.

The car rushed forward, throwing Robert against the driver's seat. Fred leaped and stuck his claw straight at the windshield, straight at Robert. He clenched his teeth and winced. The car hit Fred's legs mid-air; they thudded and wrecked the bonnet, the airbag exploded in Robert's face, and the windshield shattered, sending small shards of glass all over the seats.

His head felt dizzy and he saw stars. Five giant nails struck through the airbag, trying to get at his face. Robert arched back and avoided the massive claw swishing around blindly. It caught his jumper and tore three long scratches into his chest. He screamed and took his knife from his belt and stabbed the palm of the claw. Fred bellowed and whimpered. Robert slashed at the werewolf's forearm and fingers. Blood seeped into his jumper and ran down his belly.

The bloody claw recoiled, and Robert looked straight into Fred's malicious yellow eyes. Eyes he had never seen until tonight; attached to a face full of nothing but hatred. Salty tears dripped into his mouth as he grimaced and slammed the pedal. The car lurched forward with Fred on the bonnet. By the time Fred got his balance, Robert smashed his foot on the brake pedal. The car stopped and Fred flew like a ragdoll onto the bumpy road.

Robert accelerated again, aiming for the dazed hunk of fur and muscle clumsily trying to find its balance. Fred looked up at the massive headlights charging him, his eyes widened. *Thump.*

The car hit him square in the nose and drove over him like a rocky bank. The off-road vehicle made light work of the hurdle. When the car got over Fred, Robert reversed and drove over him again, feeling like he'd torn his heart from his chest.

The werewolf lay limp in the car's headlights, his fingers and toes twitching. The wind blew dust and debris over his body. Robert walked over the creature that used to be his dog, his best friend, Fred.

"I'm sorry, Freddy boy. I really am," Robert cried. Half of his jumper hung open and his scratch wounds stung like fire.

He knelt beside Fred and saw small plumes of steam coming from his mouth. "I'll end the pain, Freddy." He took his knife out. "It'll be over in a second." Robert plunged the knife into Fred's chest. He twitched and gasped a final breath.

Sunlight glistened in Beglik lake. Robert scratched at the bandage wrapped around his chest. The wound itched like hell. Stanil and Ogi came to check up on him after he told Ivana what happened. They wanted to investigate the strange black wolf, *Ivanwolf*, with some of the boys from the village while Robert recovered and saw to Fred.

He just finished digging out the last bit of dirt and looked over the water. Fred always liked the lake. He hauled Fred's massive body into the grave and put a note on his chest.

The note read: *Fred, I can't explain the size of the hole you've left in my life. You were my best friend, my hunting partner... my family. I remember when I could hold you in one hand. I tried to find your favorite toy, the squeaky sausage with a stupid face. I remember how you used to squeak it in the night when you were a pup, it would drive me insane. Now I find myself aching to hear that sound one more time. I couldn't find the toy. God knows where you left it.*

Anyway. You were always a good boy, Freddy, the best damn boy any man could ever ask for. A truly loyal hound, my brother in arms. Keep my seat warm up there for me, buddy. I love you.

Stanil Korabov sat by his fireplace and opened a can of Kamenitza beer and drank until his head swam and his sore muscles felt numb. Earlier today, he, Ogi, and a few other men from Malka village went to cull the werewolves that wounded the Englishman, Robert Hall, and turned his pet dog against him.

They left for the cave today after checking on Robert, getting there in the morning when the werewolves were easy pickings. Robert had warned them of the numbers, and the strange black wolf that was their pack leader, they struggled to believe it at first.

The wolf-men attacked them like frenzied animals, far more aggressive in their weakened forms than usual. When word got back to the village about the whole affair, Baba Svetla would declare the black wolf a supernatural creature, using vile sorcery to exert such influence over the werewolf pack. Stanil believed her. Some speculated it was just another werewolf.

They were deep in the cave when Stanil first saw the black wolf. He had just finished off the last few werewolves and proceeded to check further into the caverns. A pair of silver eyes appeared in the darkness, followed by two rows of teeth and a low, rumbling snarl. Robert had told him that he tried to avoid killing the wolf, thinking it a natural creature. Stanil wasn't like Robert. He shot the wolf with his hunting rifle, and the beast leaped at him, seemingly undeterred by the shot.

Stanil wrestled with it on the floor, punching it in the face and kicking its gut. Multiple layers of thick clothing guarded his arms against the wolf's teeth long enough for help to arrive. He remembered loud shots ringing to his side and the room flashing with light, revealing the black wolf in full. Ogi had put five bullets into the wolf, which was enough to make it flee into a rocky passageway, but not enough to kill it.

The group tried looking for it until they heard a terribly loud howl bouncing through the walls. They all clasped their ears, feeling like the sound might burst their eardrums. The howling didn't stop, and after a while, they felt the very floor they stood on begin to shake. The walls cracked and shards of sharp rock fell from the ceiling like spears, one of them impaled a man called Emiliyan through the chest. They all bought flowers for his wife that day. They ran out of the cave with all haste, past many werewolf corpses, hoping that would be the end of the infestation. *But we didn't get the damn wolf.*

Now he waited, hunting rifle by his side, looking out of the window in case more werewolves prowled the village. Stanil waited so long into the night that he fell asleep in his chair by the fire. He dreamt he was lying at the top of a mountain, but there were two full moons in the sky. For a moment he thought they were *looking* at him.

A hand with skin that felt like hard leather grabbed his shoulder. Stanil jumped and looked up. A man with silver eyes, long black hair with a grey streak down the side, and a mustache with curly tips looked down at him. Blood leaked from several holes in his black overcoat, which Stanil assumed to be gunshots.

"You're going to die tomorrow, Stanil," the man said. He smelt like a dog.

M.T Johnson is a writer and entrepreneur from England. He writes short stories and novels in the horror, fantasy, and speculative fiction genres, and has work published on several websites/online magazines and anthologies. A new writer who took a liking for the craft just over a year ago.

Rabbit Ears in the Laundry

Holly Barratt

The rabbit ears in the laundry seemed like such a little thing, after months of trying to look shocked at the local news, of burying corpses and the early morning drives into the country.

I've always prided myself on being open-minded. Everyone deserves love, whatever their little quirks or inclinations. We are all human after all.

Well, that's the first thing – we're not all human are we? I know some women claim men are a different species, but I never knew I was supposed to take it literally. By the time I found out what it was that made Tim so different, I was already hooked. He said he left it 'til then on purpose. He was a bit nervous of course, but mainly he wanted me to know him and love him as a man.

He was an amazingly intelligent and kind. He loved art galleries and fine wines. He had a day job as a teacher and donated more of his salary to charity than anyone else I knew. His daylight self seemed tailored to compensate for his other side. He really was the ultimate in middle class refinement, cultured to the point of parody. I loved that he quoted Shelley at me on our first date; I loved that he ate vegan food and used words like "verisimilitude".

And despite any concepts of gender roles we might have been deconstructing during dinner, he would always help me into my coat, drive me home and kiss me on the cheek before very pointedly *not* pressurising me to invite him in.

I couldn't help but feel a little insulted after a while. He never suggested spending the night together, never invited me back to his place, never let his hands venture far below my neck. I knew he wasn't religious – quite the opposite in fact. After three months I was frustrated; at six I was starting to wonder if I had the wrong end of the stick. Were we just good friends after all? Were the kisses and dinner dates just part of an affectionate, generous nature? It crossed my mind more than once that there was someone else: a wife, another girlfriend; a boyfriend – although it seemed ludicrous that I wouldn't have caught wind of something like that.

My concerns about our physical relationship started to seep into the once-valued conversations. He'd be talking about the destructive nature of love, how we're often drawn into ruin by our biological instincts and all I could do was to think how soft his lips looked. I'd enjoy the momentary flicker of his distraction as I ran the side of my foot across his ankle and drove myself a little crazy with the silky texture of the hairs there. I was aching to get past the intellectual, to discover even the slightest hint of longing.

I asked eventually. When he refused my offer of a nightcap I pursued it for once.

"I don't bite," I told him.

"I know," he said.

"Do you have a problem with intimacy Tim?" I meant to sound concerned, but it came out like an accusation.

He cracked a smile but carried on gripping the steering wheel, looking out into the night

"Oh for God's sake just come up and have a coffee," I said, and unbuckled his seatbelt.

I didn't notice any change at the time. The lights were dimmed and to be frank I was a bit preoccupied. When I look back I guess I can picture something heavier in his features, a creasing of the brows and a widening of the irises so they seemed to fill the eye sockets much more. I definitely wasn't alarmed by it anyway – even when I felt his nails, strangely long for a man, digging into the small of my back. His kisses were wet and badly aimed, but that only re-enforced my ideas that it was lack of experience bothering him. I was still disappointed when he broke away and staggered like a drunk into the kitchen.

After a few hurt and confused moments I followed, and found him reading the arts section of the previous day's paper. Verging on anger I snatched it away.

"What?" I demanded "If you don't want me for god's sake just bloody say so."

"I do," he said "But sometimes I have a bit of a problem."

"I can be patient," I said, "It'd help a lot if you'd relax."

"It's not the problem you're thinking of."

And that was where it started really. After he came out with it and I believed him. I wish he'd said something earlier – but I guess I was the only woman who really gave him any kind of support after finding out. There'd been the odd Goth girl when he was younger who thought it was cool and sexily dangerous, but no-one who accepted him as someone with their own place in nature, someone with needs and weaknesses like anyone else.

We were able to control things pretty well between us for a long time. We drew up a calendar of the lunar cycles, and bar a few minor disasters when he changed unexpectedly, we were able to predict high danger points and I'd arrange to sleep away from home to avoid impulsive mauling.

I did tours of the pet shops across three counties to keep us stocked with small furry prey and keep attacks on neighbours' dogs and children to a minimum. Stories of an unidentified "beast" were rife. Someone even caught him on video once, from a distance. But no link with the newly-wed couple in the two bedroom semi was made.

Our need to take such meticulous care for each others' needs brought us closer. Our passion was all the greater for the constraint of the rigid monthly schedule and the sense of danger. We knew beyond a doubt that our love was unique. We were the only couple I knew of who kept a loaded tranquiliser gun beside the bed.

But every adorable little quirk becomes an irritant eventually. I just looked down at the little bloody ears this morning and it struck me how normal the whole thing had become. I was pissed off about my ruined white undies, about having to scrape the mess into the bin again. My life was a pattern of mopping up entrails, sympathising with distraught neighbours, and fearing for my life in the most indifferent way one possibly can.

He's still sleeping and it's 2pm. Dried blood around his mouth and under his nails but still dark and gorgeous. I'll always think that no matter what.

But tomorrow I have to sleep away from home again, then come back and wash more remains of dead mammals off my smalls and wonder if the kids next door will be crying over the demise of another much-loved pet. It's just too much now. And I'm sorry, but at my time of life I just want a husband who doesn't turn into a monster every time the moon is full.

Holly Barratt is a writer living in Wales who primarily writes short stories in the science fiction, horror and magic realism genres. She is currently working on a novel

Rewilding

Eric Nash

In 2016, several werewolf sightings were reported along Barmston Drain in the city of Hull. The beast was known as 'Old Stinker', and the incidents made the British Press. The locals organised a werewolf hunt to catch him. They never did.

New moon (1% visible)
Hampton Mendip, Somerset, October 31st

The child in the werewolf costume stopped to look. The plastic bucket, full to the brim with rainbow-coloured sweets, quit its knocking against the kid's leg and behind, the black balloon slouched on the damp pavement. The mother, dressed as a witch from the shiny corsets coven, continued to click around the corner of Mill Way into New Road.

A man wearing a three-quarter length coat leant against the red brick of Reynold's antique shop. In the streetlight, he looked Sally's age, maybe slightly older, nearing thirty. Attractive, dark-haired, dangerous-looking but that was okay. She stopped herself; she didn't stay long in places, and relationships – even friendships – meant pain.

He had his collar up and one hand stuffed in a coat pocket, smoke drifted up from the fingertips of his other. His attention was on Sally. The kid's gaze was drawn to her too.

Sally rummaged for her keys.

The man gave the werewolf a smile, the awkward kind, and the boy ran after his mum, scattering rainbows on the concrete.

The air carried a clean, sharp chill. Sally let herself into the flat and locked the door.

Waxing crescent moon (3% visible)

The heartbeat rhythm of the commuter train threatened to rock Sally's eyes to a close as her book of collected poetry tightened round her thumb.

Out of the grimy window, the pine woodland in which she often ran lay high on the horizon keeping the land snug. Above it, the sun was rising; pale through the mist yet blessing the nearby ash and birch with copper and gold. The autumn sun made death look pretty. Leaves had just started to fall onto the rails: summer had finally burned out, its embers cooling on the earth. She knew that here in the countryside it was understood that decay had duration and purpose.

Sally checked her phone. Since several people had tweeted sightings of some sort of 'wolfman' in the area, the hashtag, HuntTheWerewolf, was getting traffic. Sally shook her head: what century did people think they were in? Best to stay at home that night, as people will be making up excuses for all sorts of silly behaviour. Sally returned to her book, her concentration broken only by snippets of conversation that prompted her to look up occasionally. After one such interlude she was aware of someone watching her.

The smile, not awkward like the previous night but easy and wide, was approaching. He had a fleck of grey hair which she had not noticed previously. A tattoo crawled out from the collar of that three quarter length coat. Definitely dangerous. She smiled back and turned the page.

The potency of Paco Rabanne stung her nostrils before he spread himself out on the vacant seat opposite. She coughed, and continued to read. There was the hint of something else underneath that chemical cloud, not soap or toothpaste, but the rich scent of mud, leaf and dew, the smell one sometimes disturbs when brushing the garden path after rain, or digging the soil. To Sally it was the smell of the woods. Maybe she was imagining it. When he eventually spoke, with an endearing Yorkshire accent, the bass timbre of his voice caused a rumbling in her chest. Her mouth twitched, she was romanticising again.

"You know when you meet someone for the first time, and then afterward you keep spotting them in places? We may have travelled together for weeks, and weren't aware of it."

"Oh, that's not creepy." She laughed. His face crumpled. "But I know what you mean." Sally also knew that he never took her train.

"I'm Matt." He leaned toward her, extending a broad, clean hand. "You're the girl from the last night."

"Sally. Hi." There was heat in his grip. "You normally hang around on street corners?"

"I was waiting for someone."

"That's a relief. Look, Matt, work on your opening lines, okay?" The blur outside slowed to form gardens and windows revealing the beginning day.

"A mate. I was waiting for a mate last night," Matt added. "I can't quite place your accent, sounds like you've spent time up north."

"Some."

"Right. Sorry for sounding weird. Nerves, I guess. I'm quite new here. Got me some work in town, no-brainer stuff. I'm a locksmith by trade, but there's nowt happening on that front."

She nodded, thought something about him picking her locks, and looked down at the page to hide her smile. She closed the book and lifted up her bag.

"Look, Sally, this is my stop, so I'll just come out with it: I'm going to the firework display on Strieber's Field this Saturday. I'd love to bump into you there."

"Nice to have met you, Matt."

As they stood, sunlight turned his eyes a curious tawny.

Waxing crescent moon (28% visible)

Warmed by a cup of spiced wine, Sally weaved through the generations of people dancing with sparklers to stand as close to the bonfire as her cheeks would allow.

Fire was complicated to Sally. As a young girl she'd sit in front of her grandfather's fireplace and watch the flames, convinced it was alive. In Strieber's Field, it was a devouring beast whose heart throbbed fast and bright; its fervour gulped in her air as it paced round and round, up and up; a beast that rode the night under a trembling moon.

Sally retreated into the crowd. And tweeted a picture of the bonfire along with the words, *Hot date tonight!* If he treated her right, they might end up in bed for a couple of hours too. Just the once.

A work colleague replied, *Oh very funny.*

No really, Savannah.

The others at Whitefell Ltd had tried to make friends with Sally, who had joined the company as a temp a month previously. All had given up except Savannah. Tonight, Sally let her defences drop, she may have been a little excited too. *His name's Matt.*

Ooh, let me know how it goes, hon.

Sally smiled. And realised how alone she'd become.

A skyrocket whooshed high into the darkness and bloomed like hogweed. When Sally levelled her gaze Matt was standing in front of her, the bonfire reflected upon the twin sheen of his eyes.

They raised cups and shared crow's feet smiles. He tucked her hair behind her ear. No man apart from her father had done that.

They stood gently leaning on each other for the rest of the display, their necks craned, the barrage of colour booming through their chests and flecks of ash brushing against their open faces. She smiled as she heard the little boy within him wonder at the finale of triumphant explosions battering the night sky.

"Can I walk you home?" he asked, lighting a fag.

Her mother would've thought his offer old-fashioned, and it did intrigue her, but they hadn't talked much and it was early enough to catch last orders. At least the invitation for a nightcap would have been flattering.

"The Huntsman's still open."

"I promised my flatmate I'd be home by ten."

"Oh."

"Yeah. He's a copper. He's on nightshift and worried that his two dogs would be *tormented* by the noise of the fireworks if they were left alone too long."

Sally had experience of police officers, they had a way of complicating matters, and she kept her distance from them. "Won't the fireworks be over by then?"

"Sorry."

"It's fine. Where do you live?"

"Five minutes down the road from your place."

"Really?" She offered him her arm. "In that case, allow *me* to walk *you* home."

A rocket exploded in the distance. She put her other hand in her coat pocket, out of the cold. His silence indicated her suggestion may not have been what he wanted.

"Okay."

Matt did most of the talking. He was nervous again. "You like poetry, don't you? When I was at school, I told one of my English teachers that I thought poetry was up its own arse. So he gave me Charles Bukowski to read. That guy really dissects, doesn't he?"

"I always thought he cleaves it wide with a blunt axe. I'm not sure how much of a favour that teacher did you; Bukowski was a misogynist and a male chauvinist."

"Possibly, or he just hated everyone."

"That was an excuse." She smiled. "Shame, I was just beginning to like you."

He squeezed her arm. "I like you too."

In the centre of town, when his fingers slipped between her own, she kept them there because it gave her the reassurance of simple times. A while later having left the people behind, they stopped outside the small Post Office where Sally regularly topped up the electric key. They were still holding on to each other. Matt's fingers touched her lobe, the faintest tug pulling her forward to meet his lips. They were cool, there was alcohol on his breath, tar in his mouth. It was just like her first kiss. The memory disentangled Sally's restraints of gravity and her consciousness became a kaleidoscope slipping starward. If she went to bed with Matt, she would come back for more. She'd been stupid.

"Matt."

He was guiding her backward into the dark doorway.

"I don't think…"

His scent was in her nostrils. His mouth was on her lips as his hand pressed against her breast through the coat. She couldn't guide the paw away. Her bag dug into her lower back. She needed to get out of there. The grip on her arse jolted Sally, and she hit the back of her head on window. He forced her against his groin so she could feel him, and bucked hard. His other hand lodged against the back of her skull.

Sally forced a burp.

"Mulled wine. Sorry. Look, you're going too fast Matt." She tried to squeeze past him, but he blocked the escape. He seemed larger than before, his eyes deeper in shadow.

The bag was loose on her hip, enabling her to slip a hand inside.

"You're teasing me," he said. His lips pursed, jaws tightened, like he was biting the inside of his mouth making a decision.

Sally clutched her keys and positioned one so it jutted out of her fist. "Let me out, Matt."

"We're not done yet." His eyes the colour of dead beech leaves fixed her. He lunged. She jabbed the key into his face and barged past him as he reeled. His hand snatched at her, nails clawed at her face, her coat.

Sally tore free and ran.

It was ten minutes to home if she cut through St Anne's churchyard, fifteen if she stayed within the safety of the streetlights. Sulphur hung in the air on the brow of Walpole Street, near the boarded-up pub, while streetlamps scattered the darkness under leaf canopies and against buildings. A couple of miles away a motorbike shifted gear. In the cloudy sky the slice of moon came and went unlike the anger Sally felt towards herself for letting this happen. She had sensed he was dangerous, and chose to romanticise this, ignoring her keen instincts because she despised them for being the offspring of fear.

The houses were set back, hedged-off from the road; St Anne's Primary squatted toad-like opposite the pitch void of a building site. She caught movement on her left side, a loping from shadow to wall to shadow. Things look different in the dark, or in the unnatural light of town, and Sally knew that perception was more volatile when one is under stress.

It was her gut that told her to hurry.

First quarter moon (37% visible)

The 7:00 a.m. alarm call brought voices other than Sally's own into her consciousness: the reporter declared the year to be the hottest on record.

It was still cold in her flat where she was already dressed in bed, having spent the night listening for sounds of Matt trying to gain entry.

Sally tried not to think what she could have done differently the previous evening. She read her book, made coffee and listened to Jon move about upstairs, and scanned the headlines, FB and Twitter on her phone instead. She saw that Jon @jonfawcett had tweeted: *7 more days to go HunttheWerewolf @ Kissing Batch Lane Hampton Nature Reserve!* And she wondered if Little Red Hood was taking the world to Hell in a picnic basket.

Throwing the phone onto the covers, Sally knew that she should be going for a run in fifteen minutes if she were serious about entering the Bristol half marathon next year. She sunk lower, closing her eyes, and there was Matt staring behind her lids.

She stamped the few paces to the bathroom. He would not control her.

Sally splashed cold water on her face, felt it sting her cheek reminding her of the raw skin that had been shredded by Matt's nails.

Bastard!

Sally put on her running shoes.

She altered all apart from the last mile of her regular run along the perimeter of Bertrand's Woods and kept within view of people. A precaution that seemed unnecessary, until the sight of him leaning against the park gates squeezed the remaining breath from her lungs.

"Sally, wait!" His voice lacked the menace it held the last time she heard it, or was it the distance that dulled its edge, separated as they were by the light Sunday traffic headed out of town.

Had he been waiting for her? She kept on running.

He was at the kerbside mirroring her pace. "Sally, look... I... I overstepped the mark."

Nearby, a man was cleaning the inside of his car, the drone of the vacuum cleaner a soundtrack to the scene she was in where lampposts and railings, hedges and walls ordered and categorised. The suburban gave the impression of safety, but it was where she'd been attacked, and where the threat lingered. Impending werewolf hunt aside, was she just as safe in the woods?

"And I want to say sorry for how I treated you last night."

Just clichéd sentiments and platitudes spilling out between his jaws like sighs.

Matt dashed across the road.

Sally spun, her hands balling into fists. "Get away!"

"I don't want to hurt you." His voice was quiet, no doubt intended to be soothing. Above his cruel, tawny eyes his sloping lids feigned sorrow.

"Leave me alone." She retreated.

The man cleaning his car frowned at them. He may come over, or at least ask if everything was all right.

"Give me a chance?"

"I did, Matt." Despite being desperate to let him know how shitty he had made her feel, continuing to engage him would only exacerbate the situation. She set a jogging pace, and resisted glancing back straightaway.

When she did, Matt had gone.

First quarter (47% visible)

Monday's commute revealed fields drowned in lakes reflecting turquoise and slate. Yet another hurricane had whip-slapped a fifty-mile long tail across the southwest. Sally preferred to watch the brittle bones of ravaged trees swaying in the gusts, or witness foolhardy drivers plough floodwaters, waves riding the tarmac. It was either that, or catch Matt staring at her from the far end of the carriage. There was no reason that she could think of why he had picked her out. He had never taken that train before they saw each other outside her flat. Was it as ridiculous as him taking payment for her spurning his advances? She just had to ride it out.

He approached when the train was click-clacking toward Sally's stop. Outside the doors, the blurred platform and its bold Brunel font signs steadied themselves with the squeal of the train's brakes. He was still ten feet away when daylight was blocked by redbrick walls; eight when a grey wave of commuters seemed to block Sally's escape. And when she knew that she would barge between the bloke carrying the rucksack and somebody on a phone, she choked on the scent of Matt's aftershave.

The doors hissed open.

"I'll be round for coffee."

Sally was left on the platform, stalled by his departing words.

Across from Sally's desk, the account manager Savannah was eating cereal. She looked up and smiled with raised eyebrows. "So how was your hot date?"

Sally shook her head, putting her bag down by her chair. "Don't ask."

"What happened?"

"It didn't go as he had planned and now he's threatening me."

"Oh shit." Savannah pushed the plastic bowl aside. "What's he said?"

"It's nothing."

"Of course it's nothing, I mean you're talking to me about it, and you never talk to anyone."

"Savannah, it's just mind-games."

"Like? Listen, this kind of shit happens a lot. Don't let the bastard get away with it."

"He knows where I live."

"Then go to the police, hon."

"Yeah." Sally preferred not being a nuisance, and had always tried to blend in with some sort of norm, however difficult that proved to be. "Anyway, how was your weekend?"

"I'm serious, Sally."

First quarter (58% visible)

She managed to ignore him throughout Tuesday's journey, travelling to and from the station in the company of other commuters. This tactic forced a detour on the return, following a couple through the new-builds on the edge of the nature reserve. The noise of the wind rushing through the trees that lined Kissing Batch Lane was like hearing the Clevedon tide drag on shingle. In front of her, the couple looked cosy, arm in arm, sloppy bobble hat and beanie, rucksack and messenger bag. It reminded Sally of her past. With the clink of a gate, the couple walked up a short path to their front door.

She hurried, blustered, like the leaves torn from the trees, and weaved through the maze of cavity-walled houses, and the litter of cars and vans spilling from drives and straddling pavements like drunks. Inviting lights and bright soundless images on large screens showed life secured by a seal of brick and glass beyond her reach. Right then, it seemed that it would always be the case.

She did not sense Matt in those last minutes.

Then she was home. Inside. Lockdown complete. Curtains drawn to shut herself away, to be forgotten.

In the dark, she lit a candle on the small table, took up a position on the cushion and did her fifteen minute meditation. Keeping control.

As she picked at her dinner of liver and – the chocolate substitute – bacon, anticipating a knock on the door, Sally scrolled through all the online advice about stalking.

Her distrust of the boys-in-blue didn't make reporting the incident an option.

She had no desire or need to speak to the stalker. The reason why he was doing this was irrelevant, and he would only lap up any attention.

Let others know. Well if she had other friends maybe that would be feasible. Jon may think she was overreacting, and he spent half the time at his boyfriend's place, anyway. Of course, now Savannah was aware, the rest of the office would be informed.

Collecting a body of proof would turn the problem into something tangible and less easy to ignore. Her counselling sessions as a teen proved writing issues down made them easier for her to process.

Protecting herself was another rule. The sites advised against weapons as these could be used against the victim. Victim. Each time Sally read the word she felt like she had been punched in the stomach.

Her fork clattered on the plate. The food was left uneaten.

Waxing gibbous (68% visible)

0645h: Woke to the stench of rotting food. A half-eaten burger and chips had been shoved through the letterbox. The contents of the wheelie bin had been emptied on to the pavement outside my door. Refuse sacks clawed apart. Jon, my neighbour, thinks it was the wind. I told him I was being stalked. He said the same as Savannah.

0730h – 0745h: He was on the train again. Far end of the carriage as always. Staring at me. That's what he does. If someone blocks his view, he shifts until he sees me. If I change my routine, it'll feel like he's won. I have no idea how long he'll keep this up?

Sally reached the end of the poem and remembered nothing because the question, why, buzzed inside her head like a trapped mozzie.

Under Matt's inspection, his violation by proxy, she put the book away and rose to meet his teeth-baring grin yellowed and sick. Sally regulated her breathing, settling the churning in her stomach and throat, as she twisted and elbowed along the carriage, intent on finding out what he thought he was doing.

He didn't look away, nor did he move back; there had been no expectation within her for him to do so, but there had been a hope. The only movements he conceded were to widen his eyes and broaden his smile.

"Hello, Sally."

"Why are you doing this?"

"Doing what?" He raised his eyebrows in mock innocence. "Travelling to work? Or, looking at your fine features?"

She knew it was wrong to have done this; she was now playing his game. "Why are you following me?"

"Only a fool," he proclaimed aloud, "would refuse to follow your beauty to the ends of the earth."

"Oh, fuck off and leave me alone."

His grin cracked. "I know what you are…" he snarled.

She took a backward step.

"… you're a tease."

1745h: He blew me a kiss as we waited on the platform. He was directly behind me as I got on the train. I wanted to punch him!

1805h: I took a taxi back home. I shall not change my routine, my life, for anyone. I will not be forced. I am not a victim.

2200h: I want this to stop.

Sally settled herself on her meditation cushion and breathed in through her nose. She would beat this, beat him. Her eyes closed. He may be outside now, leaning against the red brick. She repeated her mantra. Maybe he was outside her window. Breathe, Sally, breathe. In her mind his boots crunched on the gravel underneath her window. His breath misted the glass as he tried to peer through the gap in the curtains.

She yanked the material together and padded to the kitchen. The relief at not seeing the shape of him illuminated by the streetlamp made her smile. That no dark figures lurked beyond the light's reach almost caused her to laugh aloud. Sally lowered the blind.

By keeping the volume off and adding subtitles on the television screen she would hear anybody outside her flat. He wouldn't come, she thought, men like Matt were all talk.

Waxing gibbous (78% visible)

0730h: Matt wasn't at the station this morning ☺ I don't want to think that this over, but it may be. God! it felt SO good!!!

1047h: He's just phoned me at work. He got straight through to my direct line. He told me what he was going to do to me. I can't write the details of this; I will NOT write the details.

"Wakey, wakey!"

Sally jumped out of her seat, her knee banged against the underside of the desk. Savannah's grin at having caused that reaction was almost as wide as the hips her hands were always perched upon.

The screensaver was in full dance which meant that she must have been out of it for over ten minutes. The taste of blood was at the back of her throat and the skin felt mangled against the tip of her tongue.

"Sally, are you okay? "

"He's—"

The phone on her desk started to ring. It was an external call. Sally grabbed her bag from near her feet and managed to not quite run.

When she pushed open the door of the office building, Sally's muscles locked rigid; her stalker was entering the Tesco Express opposite.

He had not seen her. This fact established a wholly liberating sense of control for Sally. The voyeuristic pleasure was sweetened by irony, and became almost a form of revenge. Desperate to keep hold of it, she followed him in.

Grabbing a can, she pretended to read the label while he went toward the Household aisle and disappeared. She teetered, forced to realise what little power she had had been sapped from her. Sally began to count slowly. If he hadn't appeared by the time she reached five, she'd get out.

On four, Matt came into view with something in his hand. He approached the checkout, ordered a packet of cigarettes, and placed a Mars Bar on the sales counter along with a reel of Duck tape.

Sally retreated to the back of the store, looking for a door, a route, an escape from the fear that was forcing her to mutter and shake. She leant against a freezer, feeling her legs giving way, yet her instinct was to hurl the can at the nearest object. Instead, it fell from her fingers, hitting the hard tiles with a crack.

By 6pm, she'd checked into a Travelodge.

Waxing gibbous moon (87% visible)

Having pulled a sickie at work, Sally found herself hiding away. The day had been spent under the shower, and in the bar tracing her finger round the rim of her glass, or turning the pages of her book without comprehending one word. She imagined that she hadn't been threatened with rape; it wasn't that difficult in a place of anonymity and transience where you could pretend to be whoever you chose. For a time.

Waxing gibbous moon (94% visible)

Her legs were stiff, stretched out on the white sheets as she leaned against the wall mounted headboard of the hotel bed. She uncrossed them and considered another day caged, staring at life beyond a dirty window.

The isolation of a hotel room was almost akin to achieving a semi-meditative state. More than once Sally had believed it possible that either her stalker was a figment of her imagination, or he had given up, yet she knew that by stepping out of this limbo into the season's chill would bring torment. She snorted at this, questioning what exactly it was that she thought she was experiencing if not torment.

According to Twitter, the world continued to spin without her input. More storms: natural and unnatural, global, and in Hampton Mendip. *Don't be scared anymore. Join us! HuntTheWerewolf HamptonNatureReserve.*

The phone in her hand beeped. An incoming text from a number she didn't recognise: "Your neighbour seems nice. Has he had you? I bet he has. Time's nearly up, Sally."

Full moon (99% visible)

When Sally decided what to do, she switched on her phone; there were forty two new messages waiting for her, from him. They were deleted immediately.

The TV was showing that morning's Remembrance service at the Cenotaph as, outside, darkness settled in the streets that channelled knots of people toward the Nature Reserve.

She was shocked that people actually believed in werewolves nowadays. Stills from an old horror movie, of angry mobs stirring hysteria with pitchforks, their faces monstrous with rallying chants, created the scene for her at the Nature Reserve. Yet the photos and footage uploaded on to social media portrayed a much darker vision.

It was a carnival crowd that gathered for the hunt that November evening. Excitement murmured through the masses clad in their Craghoppers or Northface kits. Adults clutched mulled wine in plastic beakers, their offspring snatching at bags of candyfloss. Vendors scuffed along the path, pushing jittery trolleys heavy with flashing swords and glowing snowflakes on sticks. One, with down-turned lips and fingerless gloves, gripped a bobbing bush of silvery balloons and shouted, "'Hunt the Wolf' stickers only three quid!"

The same slogan was visible on a rally of banners as beams of torchlight strobed across the wetlands; a loudhailer was brandished; the long barrel of a shotgun pointed toward the very bright and very large moon.

Sally paced the room with frustration cramping her muscles.

She sent him a text.

Full moon (100% visible)

There was no guarantee that Matt would come. He probably thought it a set up and the police would be there waiting for him. There had been no response to the text she sent last night, nor had she heard from him all day. It didn't matter now: she would see him tonight regardless.

Her apartment was in darkness when she returned, leaving the door unlocked behind her. Along with a lingering staleness, a few circulars lay on the floor of the hallway, and her drawers were still hanging open from her rushed exit during the previous week. No sound came from Jon upstairs.

Behind the blind, she burned the few diary entries she had scribbled on notepaper. That done, she removed her clothes and returned them folded to the drawers which she then closed, and padded through to the living room. The fading light of dusk illuminated her skin as she pushed the curtains open.

Placing the cushion in the middle of the room, she knelt and waited for the moon to show and the tide to rise inside her.

Sally could feel it already. As always it began in her stomach like excitement, and spread through her nerves, tingling her chest, her limbs, her entirety. She'd then have the urge to vomit; a physical manifestation of her loathing. Thick hairs would appear covering the human downy ones, the first visible signs before the pain, the bone-breaking agony she had to endure.

Tonight, she welcomed it. Tonight, she would become free.

Eric Nash is a member of the Horror Writers' Association. Over a dozen of his short stories have appeared in Aggregate by Writerfield, Demain Publishing's Short Sharp Shocks series, Mythic and other magazines and anthologies.

The Lodger

Laura Garrity

Our lodger Mr. Pendle was urinating on the forsythias again. Cal climbed up next to me on the window seat, standing on it to see what I was looking at. "Sophie, he's doin' it again!" he mumbled around his thumb.

He had his back to us, but it was pretty clear what he was doing. "Yep, sure is."

"Can I pee outside?"

"You better not, Mom won't like it."

"Then why can Mr. Pebble do it?"

"Pendle. He shouldn't either. Maybe he's drunk."

"Does that mean he can't use the toilet?"

"No, he just doesn't know what he's doing is all."

Part of me doubted that. It looked like what he was doing was very precise for a drunk. And he hadn't fallen over, like Daddy used to do when he had too much. Mr. Pendle had fallen up our steps when he first came to stay - Mom had found him laid out on the porch clutching her newspaper ad about the room for rent in one grubby hand. She had scowled at him, and looked like she was about to turn him away, but he apologized so sweetly she agreed to let him stay.

Mom said he hadn't a soul in the world, and she felt bad for him. But I also suspected that her forgiveness might have had a bit to do with the big stack of envelopes marked final notice on the hall table.

Outside, Mr. Pendle turned toward the house. I ducked back behind the curtains, but Cal waved. He was too little to know he shouldn't spy on folks. Mr. Pendle waved back, and a few minutes later I heard the back door bang shut as he came back into the house. I hoped that Cal didn't start peeing in the yard, or Mom was going to throw a fit.

Mr. Pendle spent most of the night alone in his room, except for supper. On the first of every month he would set a check beside Mom's dinner plate, which she would quietly slip into her skirt pocket when she sat down to eat. Mr. Pendle seemed to like Mom's cooking, but he didn't talk much during dinner. He would answer questions put to him, and sometimes I saw him smiling down at his plate when Cal said something goofy. He was about Mom's age, I figured, and it had occurred to me once or twice that he might be what Mom would call handsome. He had a heavy jaw, and his eyes were an interesting greenish brown color behind his glasses. He looked weathered, like he spent a lot of time working outside, but he said that he'd been a mechanic, before he had to "move on". I tried to ask him once what he'd moved on from, but Mom shushed me, and piled more broccoli on my plate. I figured it was one of those things that it wasn't polite to ask - it seemed like there were a lot of those things.

When I got up in the middle of the night to use the bathroom, mom's bedroom light was on. I heard what sounded like a laugh, but not a nice laugh. I padded over and peeked through the door. Mom sat up against the headboard, blankets covering her lap. She saw me, and gave a sniff, rubbing the back of her hand across her eyes.

"Are you ok, honey? It's late."

"I just had to go to the bathroom."

"OK. Be quiet so you don't wake up Cal."

"I won't." I stood and stared at her for a moment. "Is everything OK?"

She gestured wearily to the bills strewn across the quilt. "Just trying to sort out what's what."

"Can't you just tell them we don't have the money?"

"Oh, Sophie. That's not true. We're just a bit behind at the moment. I've got to get this all organized is all - and some of these are copies of the same bills, they just keep sending them over and over again."

"Mr. Pendle has money - maybe he can pay it."

Mom sniffed again, but gave a weak smile. "Well, he's already paying rent, see? I use that to pay the bills. That's how *that* works."

I shuffled my feet, feeling sleepy again. "Oh, right."

"We'll be fine, honey. Don't you worry about this - it's not your problem, OK? Get on back to bed now."

I nodded, and went back to bed, but I couldn't seem to get back to sleep.

A few days later, Cal and I were playing circus in the backyard. I was the ringmaster, and he was the lion jumping through my hula hoop over and over again. He stopped all of a sudden, and whimpered "Sophie, that's a wolf". He pointed toward the bushes at the edge of the yard. I turned to look, ready to tell him that there was nothing there. Mom said that Cal had a lot of imagination and still enough of a baby in him that he got confused sometimes. He woke me up a lot with his bad dreams, and it took a while sometimes to convince him the monsters weren't real.

I was so surprised when I saw it that I froze. Sure enough a gray wolf was slinking under the shrub and staring at us with wild yellow eyes. It was like my brain had shut off and I couldn't move or yell or anything. Cal grabbed my arm and tugged. "Sophie, Sophie, we gotta go inside! Now!"

My feet moved and soon I was dragging him along by the arm toward the back porch. My lungs opened up and I shouted "Mom! Help!"

She met us in the mudroom. "Sophie, what's wrong?"

She scooped Cal up into her arms and I followed her into the kitchen where Mr. Pendle sat at the table eating a turkey sandwich.

"There's a wolf!" Cal cried, "Mama -a wolf in the yard!"

Mom put Cal down and wiped her hands on her apron. "Oh, honey, I don't think so - it's probably just the Jefferson's dog on the loose again. There haven't been wolves around here for a long time."

"But it was! Wasn't it, Sophie?"

I thought it was, but Mom seemed so sure of herself, and I didn't want to seem like a baby. I shrugged. "I guess it could have been a big dog."

"It wasn't Mooney, Mooney's red," Cal insisted, "It was a gray wolf!"

Mr. Pendle got up from the table and looked out the kitchen window. "You saw a wolf out there?"

Cal started to sniffle. "It WAS a wolf!" he insisted. "It looked just like in the books."

Mr. Pendle hunched down and offered Cal a handkerchief. "You said it was gray?"

Cal sniffed into the handkerchief and nodded.

"What did its nose look like?"

"Kind of pointy."

Mr. Pendle nodded gravely and Mom sighed. "You really shouldn't encourage him..." she began.

He stood up with a grunt. "You know it really might be one. People keep building, and you'll see lots of things that used to stick to the woods. Where was it, son?"

"Near the flower tree."

"The forsythia bush, with the yellow flowers," I corrected.

"Did it come past the shrubs into the yard?"

Cal shook his head. "It was under them."

"Well that's fine, probably could hear there were people around. They don't like to come to close to folks if they can help it."

I noticed that for the rest of the day, I kept seeing Mr. Pendle peeking out the curtains into the yard.

Sometimes when I got annoyed with Cal I would hide on him. It wasn't very nice, but sometimes I just needed time to think, or play on my own. I was up in the big oak tree playing army fort when Mr. Pendle came out of the house and walked all the way out to the back fence. A few minutes later a woman arrived. Her hair hung in two long braids and she was barefoot. She seemed about the same age as Mr. Pendle - not old, but the sunlight picked out some gray in her dark brown hair. I held myself still, and peeked down through the branches.

"I thought it was you," he said quietly, "You shouldn't have come, the kids saw you. You scared the little one."

"I needed to get you a message. I hoped you would be the only one who saw me."

"What message?"

"The manifestation. It will be here soon."

"I know - I can feel it, same as you."

"It's a strong one." She pointed her chin toward the house. "Don't get distracted."

"I don't reckon it will be more than I can handle. But thank you for your concern," he said bitterly.

She looked behind her quickly, then turned back to him and gripped the fence. "I've missed you, William. I was worried - please don't be angry."

"I'm not angry. I know how things are. I'm just sorry I let you down."

"It wasn't a fair challenge. He's ten years younger than you, it's not right."

He turned back to her, and put his hand on top of hers. "There's no use thinking like that. We knew this could happen someday."

"There are others in the pack who think -"

"Don't. The pack has to stay together. That's just the way things are. Us fighting among ourselves and getting distracted is exactly what *they* want."

"I know. William - you'll be careful?"

He nodded and watched her walk off toward the road.

Later, I wiped a layer of dust off our dictionary and looked up manifestation.

> man·i·fes·ta·tion
> Noun
> 1. an event, action, or object that clearly shows or embodies a theory or an abstract idea.
> 2.a symptom or sign of an ailment.

Was Cal getting sick? I sat down to play Tinker Toys with him, and it didn't seem like anything was wrong with him, aside from being put out that I had disappeared on him for a while. I put my hand on his cheek like Mom did when we were sick, but his skin felt normal and he pushed my hand away.

The next day, I found Mr. Pendle in the front yard, snipping away at the hedges with Dad's rusty old clippers that looked like giant scissors. Without saying anything, I grabbed the rake from the porch and started to clean up the trimmings. He took off his hat and waved it at his sweaty face. "Thanks, that'll save some time out in this heat."

"I don't mind," I told him. He ruffled my hair and went back to work.

"There was a book in the library," I told him, "where the hedges were all cut like animals."

"It's called topiary," he said.

"Yeah - can we make this a topiary?"

He smiled and ran his hand across the top of the shrubs. "I don't think your mother would appreciate it. And I'm not sure if you have quite enough hedges here to work with."

"We could make a wolf, to scare away that other wolf."

He went still. "Are you afraid of that wolf? It won't hurt you - just don't get too close if you see it again. It's a wild thing. It'll protect itself, but it doesn't mean any harm."

"I'm not scared!"

"Oh, beg your pardon! I'm sure it's just Cal."

"He has bad dreams sometimes."

"About wolves?"

"Sometimes - or monsters, or people yelling."

"What kind of monsters?"

"I don't know - he just says it's a twisty monster. Sometimes Cal says crazy stuff."

"Poor little guy - just probably doesn't know the word for what he's trying to say. It'll be easier when he's older. *Twisty*? That's what he said?"

"He said it was like smoke, but not."

"Huh. That's quite a dream."

I raked everything in a neat pile, then waited for more snippings to build up, since it was more fun that way. "Who was that lady yesterday?" I asked suddenly. I could almost hear Mom telling me to mind my bee's-wax.

He looked surprised, but he answered. "That's a lady I know from before I lived here. Her name is Gwen."

"She's pretty."

"I suppose folks might say so."

"Is she nice?"

He looked over at me with an exasperated grin and waggled his hand in a "sort of" gesture.

"Where did you live before?"

"A group of us lived way out in the country."

"Like a farm?"

"More like the woods."

"Why did you leave?"

"Well, that's complicated grown up stuff, but basically, I got into a fight and I lost so I had to go."

"Did you say you were sorry?"

"No - it wasn't that kind of fight."

"I'm glad you're here though."

"Me too."

I started raking again, leaning over to get at the little bits around the base of the hedges. I kept feeling a tickle and looked up to find that Mr. Pendle was purposely cutting so the bits of leaves fell on my head. I picked the pieces out of my hair and threw them into my pile, rolling my eyes at him.

He stopped and wiped his face with his handkerchief. "Hey, Sophie, what happened to your dad?"

"He ran away from home when Cal was a baby."

"I'm sorry - that's a hard break."

I shrugged. "It's ok - Mom takes good care of us."

"She's a good woman." Not fancy words, but the way Mr. Pendle said it made it sound like it was the highest praise he could think of.

"She's still pretty for her age," I offered, which was something I had overheard other ladies say about her.

He stifled a chuckle behind his hand. "I suppose she is," he agreed.

We finished with the hedges, and he ran his hand along the perfectly flat top with a glow of pride. "Look at that," he said, "perfectly level."

I couldn't reach the top, but ran my hand along the flat edge. "Perfect," I agreed, "I think we deserve lemonade."

"That does sound good right about now. I'll get cleaned up and meet you in the kitchen."

While Mr. Pendle took a shower, I showed Mom what

we had done, and she was thrilled to have the front of the house looking so neat. I woke Cal from his nap, and by the time Mr. Pendle came to the kitchen Mom had fixed a big pitcher of lemonade and even cut up some strawberries from the back garden.

The phone rang while Cal and I were at the table eating cereal at the kitchen table. Mom looked worried as she cradled the phone in her shoulder, and fumbled through the junk drawer for a pen and paper. "Oh Minnie, I'm so sorry - of course I'll try and get there just as quick as I can. I just need to sort out something with the kids... Ok, give me that address again?" She paused and scribbled on the paper. "I'm so sorry, I'll be there just as soon... ok... ok. See you soon."

She turned and jumped when she saw me standing there. "What's happened?" I asked.

"Oh, honey, do you remember cousin Minnie who came last summer? Her mother is very sick, and she thinks I should come see her."

"Oh. Do me and Cal have to go?"

"Cal and I," she corrected wearily.

"Do we?"

"I don't think you can come to the hospital, I'll have to find someone to stay with you."

"Why? Mr. Pendle's here."

"Shush! I'm sure Mr. Pendle has things to do."

Mr. Pendle of course chose that moment to come down the stairs. "Is something wrong?" he asked.

"Oh, we have a bit of a family emergency. I'll have to be gone overnight, but I'll call Mrs. Johansson to take the kids. Sophie - can you get out the suitcase from the hall closet?"

"It's too big," I whined.

"It's empty, Goose, you can lift it."

"I can stay with kids," Mr. Pendle offered, "It's no trouble at all." Mom's face must have shown some doubt, because he added, "I had lots of little brothers and sisters. I expect we can get by."

"Oh, I don't know, it's nothing personal, but Cal can be tricky..."

"Am not!" Cal squealed.

"I can help take care of Cal," I said. I didn't want to stay with Mrs. Johansson, she was cranky and not a very good cook.

"Whatever you think is right," Mr. Pendle said.

"Sophie - what did I say about that suitcase?"

Begrudgingly I went to get the suitcase from the closet, and left it in Mom's room so she could pack her things. By the time I got back, it was settled that Mr. Pendle would watch us and Mom would be back the next night.

That night I had trouble falling asleep knowing Mom wasn't there. When I finally did sleep, I had a nightmare. There were a bunch of kittens trapped in a hole under the porch, mewing. But whenever I went to pick one up and take it to safety, it would slip through my fingers like water. I started awake, and realized that the noise had not been a litter of kittens, but Cal crying in his room. I padded quietly down the hall, and the wood floor was so cold it burned the soles of my feet. The breath from my mouth came out in puffs of smoke, like when I played outside in the snow, except it was July.

As I got closer to the room, I heard a low growl coming from Cal's room and I froze. I pictured the wolf from the yard climbing through his window, flattening itself to squeeze through, jaws dripping in the moonlight. I peeked around the doorway, and the wolf stood on Cal's bed, just as I had imagined. But instead of eating Cal, the wolf stood between him and silvery shadow in the corner snarling and snapping. Its ears pointed forward and its hair stood on end in a way that reminded me of our old cat Jingles when she was about to snap at me. Cal's arms were wrapped around the wolf's back leg as he sobbed into its fur. The silver shadow spun itself into a pillar, which slowly turned into a man shape, with horns on his head. He turned toward my brother, eyes glowing blue.

I stepped in the door, and yelled the first thing I thought of from Sunday school. "GO AWAY! GO AWAY IN THE POWER OF JESUS!"

It didn't explode into mist or anything like I thought it would. It just turned toward me, and stared.

The wolf took advantage of the momentary distraction to leap at the shadow-man. I climbed up on the bed beside Cal and we wrapped our arms around each other. The wolf bit at the air, jaws snapping on seemingly nothing. Finally it seemed to catch hold of something of substance, and shook its powerful neck back and forth. The shadow man let out a wail that shook the walls, and I covered my ears. The wolf's jaw opened wide, and it gobbled the shadow down in several giant bites. It looked back and Cal and me with moss green eyes, then let out a whine and fell over on his side.

Cal scrambled out of bed and knelt on the floor beside the wolf, laying his head on its heaving ribs. He looked at me eyes wide. "Is he poisoned?"

I shook my head. "I don't know. Maybe he needs water?"

Cal ran to the bathroom down the hall, and returned with the little cup he used to brush his teeth. I was about to tell him it was too small, but the wolf managed to lap up the water with its tongue just fine. I took the blanket from the bed, and laid it over the wolf. Then we both lay down beside him to watch over him, and fell asleep like that on the floor.

I woke up on the floor next to Cal, with the blanket spread over us. I smelled bacon in the kitchen and my stomach growled. I woke Cal up, although I would usually be pretty eager to get to the bacon before him. But I wasn't quite ready to leave him alone yet. It was a bright sunny day, and already warm. Seeing the sun streaming through the lace curtains leaving familiar patterns on the floor, and the smell of bacon in the kitchen suddenly made me doubt my memory from the night before.

We padded into the kitchen and found Mr. Pendle cooking not just bacon but eggs and sausages too.

He made Cal and I plates and set them at the table. He acted friendly enough but would quite look me or Cal in the eyes. "You sleep ok?"

I nodded and exchanged one of my bacon pieces for the sausage on Cal's plate, since I knew he wouldn't eat them. Mr. Pendle sat down, and I noticed his plate was almost overflowing. He dug into the eggs like he was starving. I stared at him, his green eyes flashing through his glasses. He looked up at me finally. "It won't be back," he said shortly.

"How do you know?"

"The wolf ate it," Cal reminded me.

"That's right," Mr. Pendle said quietly, "The wolf ate it, and now it won't trouble you anymore."

Satisfied with that answer, and having eaten the bacon, Cal scampered off to play leaving his plate half full. Mom would never have let him get away with it, but Mr. Pendle didn't seem to mind. He just put his head back down over his breakfast.

"Was it poison?" I asked. I had read about poison in Mom's mystery books.

"Something like that."

"It looked like it hurt."

He took of his glasses and rubbed at the bridge of his nose. He looked younger without them. "I'm sorry you saw that. That you were scared."

"But what was it?"

"It's hard to explain – it's a creature of corruption. Remember how we talked about the wolf, and how it was just wild, but didn't want to harm anybody?"

I nodded.

"What you saw, it's not like that. They want to do harm to the world on purpose. They just like pain. And there are certain people that are like the opposite of that, they have a special gift to bring good things to the world, so those entities, they try to destroy them."

"It came to kill Cal?"

"More like to corrupt him. What you saw- that took a lot of energy. And people like me can feel that energy, see?"

"Wolf people?"

"That's right. We're protectors - our job is to watch for these energies, and to stop the manifestations. I never intended for you to see that. I thought when it eventually happened I could probably convince Cal that it was a nightmare, and put his mind at ease."

"I'm too smart for that."

He smiled. "Yes."

"I wasn't afraid of you –I knew you were protecting us."

"I'm glad."

I thought some more, chewing on my lip. "Cal is going to do something special?"

"I hope so. He can if he wants, when he's grown."

"What about me?"

"I think you'll make a very good protector. That's very important too."

"Can I be a wolf?"

"I'm afraid not. That has to be something you're born

with."

I sighed. "I guess that's for the best. Mom would get pretty worried. You're not going to leave are you?"

He got up and started gathering the plates. "No – don't worry about that. I'll be here to keep an eye on things."

"Good. We like you here. And Mom does too."

He blushed a bit, then turned away and went to the sink to start on the dishes.

All that summer, the monster didn't come back. I wondered if Cal had just been that confident in the wolf's protection, or if he had truly *known* through some special gift of his. But what did happen, just as the nights were starting to get cold and the fireflies were winking out for the season, was that Daddy came back. He turned up a bit after dinner and parked his car half on the driveway and half on the lawn. He ran up to the house and pounded the door and shouting about Mom taking up with some man. She opened the door to try and get him to shush, but wasn't letting him come in the house. I saw Cal peeking down from the top of the stairs with wide eyes, and the only thing I could think of was to run and get Mr. Pendle.

He was already outside his door when I got upstairs. He put his hand on my shoulder. "Go keep an eye on your brother," he said calmly, as he tucked his glasses in his pocket.

I tugged at his elbow. "Don't eat him," I whispered.

He glared in the general direction of the ruckus. "Don't worry it's not that kind of situation. He's not evil, just *confused*."

Mr. Pendle started down the stairs, and I went to Cal and held on to him while we watched through the railing.

"Is there a problem?" Mr. Pendle asked.

"I'm so sorry about the noise," Mom said, "It's just a misunderstanding."

"You *him*? The man they're all saying has been living here with *my* wife and *my* kids?" Daddy grunted.

"I imagine so."

"Suppose we step outside then!"

"Suppose we do?"

Mom gasped. "Oh, Mr. Pendle, you don't have to explain anything, he's very drunk and…"

"I understand, Ma'am. I know what *he* is." He looked at Daddy and pointed toward the door. "Well?"

They went into the yard, and I dragged Cal to the window so we could watch. I couldn't make out what they were saying anymore, but I could tell that Daddy was shouting and Mr. Pendle was just as calm as could be. Suddenly Daddy snapped and ran right at him, head down like a bull. As he came near, Mr. Pendle lashed out like a snake and flipped Daddy off his feet onto his back. As he lay twitching on the ground, Mr. Pendle knelt beside him, said something in his ear and walked back into the house. Mom stood on the porch with her arms folded across her chest. Then, to my amazement, Mom walked over to where Daddy was flopping on the ground like a fish and kicked him once in the side before running back into the house herself. I thought Daddy might be hurt, or dead, but after a minute he got up and limped to his car then peeled out of the driveway without looking back.

I heard Mom yelling and snuck downstairs, Cal following behind like a little shadow. I peeked around the kitchen door, and saw Mom pacing back and forth, throwing her arms in the air.

Mr. Pendle put his glasses back on. "I was just trying to help. In my experience his type doesn't respond to talk."

"I *know* how to handle him, you shouldn't have done that! Two grown men fighting on the lawn - do you know what they'll all be saying now? This isn't some roadhouse, Mr. Pendle!"

"I'll apologize to him, try and smooth things over if that's what you want."

She sighed and crossed her arms over her chest. "Not particularly."

"I'm sorry I embarrassed you, I didn't think of that. I should have let you handle it."

"Yes, you should have. I don't see where it's any concern of yours."

"I couldn't stand there and let him say those things about you. I guess I just saw red."

"*Why*, for heaven's sake?"

He leaned forward and clutched the back of one of the kitchen chairs. "Because you're a kind person, and you work hard to take care of those kids, with no help from anyone. And you've been handed a bad lot, but you've still got joy in you, and anyone who doesn't respect someone like you, well, they're no kind of man. That's my opinion on it."

Mom looked up at him, and her face turned pink. "*Oh.*"

He glanced away. "Well."

She put her hand on top of his. "You're not hurt, are you?"

"No, I'm fine."

Mom started to say something else but then caught sight of Cal and me in the doorway. She rushed over to hug us. "Everything's going to be OK," she said.

Cal patted her face. "I know, Mama."

"You're not going to make Mr. Pendle leave, are you?" I asked.

Mr. Pendle coughed and looked away, and Mom chuckled. "No, he can stay. But there won't be any more fighting, so you don't have to worry about that."

Cal squirmed away and climbed up on the chair. He reached up and tugged Mr. Pendle's face so they were eye to eye. "No fighting. Be good," he said, and I realized he was talking right to the wolf.

"I promise," Mr. Pendle said solemnly. Cal nodded, satisfied, climbed down from the chair and ran off to play. And I knew it was the truth, because a wild creature would defend its home, but didn't really mean to harm anyone.

Laura Garrity is a writer from Connecticut, USA. She studied creative writing at Hofstra University, and is a member of the Fairfield County Writers Group and The Written Word writers' group at the MAC. Her work is sometimes Sci-Fi/Fantasy, sometimes Horror and sometimes just odd.

The Wolf is Always at Your Door

EJ Sidle

I wake up face-down with a .45 digging into my ribs. For a long moment I can't remember where I am, then I recognise the worn upholstery. I'm stretched out across the front seat of my car, gun in my jacket pocket, and the cheery sign of a 24-hour diner looming in the rear-view mirror.

It's after sunrise, but still early enough that it's quiet. I scrub a hand over my face, waiting for my head to stop spinning. I'd been out late last night celebrating a successful hunt. Werewolves aren't always the easiest to take down, sometimes it doesn't go according to plan. Not this time, though. This time it had been easy. Another dead wolf, another collected bounty, another bar drunk dry. Same old story.

The hangovers are new, though. Maybe I'm getting old.

My phone rings, loud and obnoxious. Wincing, I grope along the dashboard until I find it. I don't recognise the number, and I sit up properly before answering. "Someone better be dying."

"Someone's *always* dying," a familiar voice responds.

"Timothy?"

"So formal," he teases. "How's it going, Con?"

"Whole lot better if you're calling," I say, too honest by far. "Been too long. It's good to hear your voice, Tim."

"Hold that thought," he says. "I need a favour."

"And what sort of favour can a lowly Wolfhunter do for a big, bad witch?" I ask, just to hear him laugh. God, I've missed his laugh.

There's not a whole lot I wouldn't do for Tim. He knows it, and he knows that I know it. Not that he needs anything from me – Tim's old magic, *proper* magic, the kind that comes without a curse. He's easily the best friend I've ever had. Once, he was a little bit more than that, too. Sometimes still is, if wolves bring me back round to his county. It never lasts, though – witches need a home, somewhere permanent to grow their powerbase. And Wolfhunters need paying bounties.

So we're friends, except for all the ways that we're not.

"It's the sort of favour I really should ask in person," Tim continues. "Where are you?"

"Kansas."

"Still driving that junker with the bench seats?"

"Hey now," I protest. "You like the benches."

"Sure I do." There's a grin in his voice, an old memory I want to follow, but then he sighs. "Just go easy on the trigger, 'kay?"

He hangs up. I start redialling, then all at once I'm not alone. My gun is in my hand before I can think about it, up and pointing at the figure slouching in my passenger seat.

"Ugh, I am not doing *that* again," Tim groans, head lolling back against the seat.

"What the *fuck*?" I demand, gun still up, finger on the trigger. "Tim?"

"Teleportation spell," he explains, infuriatingly unconcerned about the gun in his face. I lower it with a growl, and he grins with a hint of ferocious, infectious joy. "Aren't you glad to see me?"

"Always."

He keeps grinning. "Good, I—"

"What in the hell is going on?" I interrupt. He exhales softly, pinching the bridge of his nose, and I notice the bruises on the underside of his wrist. "You hurt?"

He scoffs. "Buy me breakfast and I'll tell you all about it."

Tim drowns his pancakes in syrup. I can't decide if I want to tangle our feet together under the table, or make a snide comment about his diet. In the end, I settle for taking a fortifying sip of coffee. I don't reach for his hand.

"These are good," he says, mouth full, syrup drooling down his chin. "Want some?"

"Tim. Why'd you zap yourself halfway across the country?" I ask. "I know that sort of magic doesn't come cheap. Not even for you."

He sighs, pushing his plate away. "I need help." He makes a complicated gesture with his hands, then aims a finger gun at my coffee. "Drink."

I do, and nearly choke on a mouthful of bourbon. "*Really?* Change it back."

"You're gonna need it," Tim mutters. Gingerly, he rolls up one of his sleeves. The bruises trail up the underside of his forearm. And, in the crook of his elbow, there are jagged teeth marks.

I know that sort of bite. I've seen it a hundred times before. "You're a *werewolf*?!"

I can't pull my gun in a diner, not even a diner that's almost empty. Which is why he wanted me in here. *Fuck.*

"I'm not!" Tim says. I stare at him, and he shrugs. "Well, not until the full moon, anyway."

He takes a deep breath. "And before that happens, you're going to kill me."

The thing about Tim is that he's always felt like *home.* When I imagine my future, after I'm done with the wolves and the road, he's always in it. Most times, he *is* it. There's never been anything else, never been any*one* else, not even when we go months without speaking. He's my sure thing, my fixed point, the love of my goddamn life.

It's not supposed to end with my bullet in his chest.

Tim doesn't look like a dead man. Instead, he just looks like he always does. I steal glances at him as we get onto the highway, watching the way he leans his forehead against the passenger window.

"Ask me," he says eventually, eyes closed. "I know you want to."

"How'd it happen?" I say.

He shrugs. "Same way it always does. Wrong place, wrong time."

"Did you tell the Coven?"

"They'll kill me if they find out."

"Which is different from me doing it?" I demand. *"Tim!"*

"If it's another witch, they get my power!" Tim snaps. "God, Connor! You think I want to be here? I don't know what lycanthropy will do to my magic, and I'll be damned if one of the Coven tries to harvest."

"Timmy."

"Imagine if a rival witch tried slurping up my power and somehow got a serve of lycanthropy on the side," he continues. "They'd torture me for it. Make it slow, make it *hurt*, in case they could wring any last drops of magic from me."

"They'd torture you?" I say, low and dangerous.

"In creatively horrible ways," he confirms quietly. "I think...I think having a Wolfhunter turning me into a pretty corpse would be far preferable. Win-win."

"How do I win?" I whisper.

Tim sighs, curling tighter on himself. "You get to spend time with me. Until it happens."

"You want to…. What? Hang out until I shoot you at the full moon?" I demand.

"No!" he says. "I want to hang out until you shoot me at a *surprise* time, before the full moon."

"Surprise time," I repeat, eyes on the road, refusing to look at him.

"I don't want to know when it's going to happen," he whispers. "Just that it will. Fast and clean, before I turn. Before I'm not me anymore."

"You're a real asshole, asking me to do it," I snap.

"I know," he says softly. "I know."

He falls asleep near the state line. There are silver bullets in my .45, and I aim at his heart.

I can't pull the trigger.

"I found you a job," Tim says, somewhere in Colorado. He's stretched out across the front seat, toes digging under my thigh as I drive. "Two mutilated corpses, and dead cattle before that."

"Might not be a wolf thing," I say.

"It is," he insists, eyes on his phone.

"Because your witchy powers say so?" I tease.

"Yeah? Blow job says I'm right."

I glance over at him, but he doesn't look up.

"Okay, you're on."

It is a wolf thing. Teenaged girl. She begs for mercy, promises that she's learning to control it even as she stands among the corpses of her family.

Tim stares at her with wide, horrified eyes.

I shoot her twice in the heart. I don't regret it.

"Maybe you'll be able to learn," I say one night, back against the door and my legs kicked across the front seat. "To control it, I mean."

"No one ever controls it," Tim says. He's stretched out in the back, staring at me from the opposite side of the car. "Why would I be any different?"

"You're probably the most powerful witch I know."

"I'm *definitely* the most powerful witch you know," he says. "What does that matter?"

"So, maybe you'll be okay."

"How many wolves have you killed?" he demands suddenly. "Hundreds?"

"Yes," I admit. "Maybe more."

"Did any of them have control?"

"No."

"Did they deserve to die?"

"They were dangerous," I defend. "They ate people, Tim."

"So they deserved it?"

"Yes, okay? They did."

He sighs. "You can't have it both ways, Con. Either wolves are killers who don't have control, or they're not. I'm not some special case just because you're in love with me."

"Don't," I whisper.

"You're going to have to kill me, Con," he says. "Just like all the others."

"Tim, I —"

"If you think you can save me, then you could have saved all the rest, too," he adds, vicious now. "That's a whole lot of blood on your hands, Connor. Maybe it's not the wolves who are the monsters."

I'm out of the car before he finishes the sentence. He doesn't try to stop me.

Hours later, I crawl back into the front seat. Tim's still in the back, curled beneath one of my jackets.

"Sorry," he mumbles as I close the door. "Didn't mean it."

"Yes you did."

We stay silent for a long time, listening to each other breathe. Finally, I squeeze my eyes shut. "Are you scared?"

"Are you?" he counters.

"Yeah," I admit. "I don't think I can do it, Timmy."

"You don't have a choice," he says. "I… *need* you to do it."

"I know."

"And, I love you too, you know?"

"Yeah, I do."

"I'm scared," he whispers, so soft I nearly miss it. "Con. Connor. I'm just so scared."

"Yeah," I say, swallowing against the lump in my throat. "I know."

I've been a Wolfhunter for most of my life, and I've seen the ways lycanthropy takes hold. Sometimes, it's all violence and anger, a rampage that lasts until the first full moon. Sometimes, it's a fever and nausea, something that could be a simple stomach flu if not for the final transformation.

Tim doesn't get angry, or sick. Instead, he gets tired. At first it's barely noticeable, just him napping against my shoulder on the stretches of highway between towns. He sleeps later each morning, passing out earlier each night. He doesn't mention it, doesn't say anything, but there's a resignation in his eyes as he stares at the stars each evening.

We both pretend we can't see the moon in the sky, and that we aren't quietly counting down the days.

"Do you ever get lonely?" Tim asks. We're in the middle of nowhere, cruising along a straight stretch of highway with the radio humming in the background.

"Hmm?"

"Doing this." He waves his hands, encompassing the road. "Bouncing between towns. No address. No family. Just wolves."

"Sometimes, yeah," I admit. "But I don't think I'm a white picket fence kinda guy."

"You know, I did the whole picket fence thing," Tim says, looking out the window again. "It was pretty lonely, too."

Two days later, I kiss him.

"That's a complication," he says, grinning. "I thought we weren't gonna do this again?"

"Don't have to," I tell him, words muffled against the skin of his throat.

He laughs, arms around my neck. "Oh no, I definitely want to," he says. "Just probably would have been easier if we didn't."

"Sorry," I say, but I don't mean it.

We spend hours tangled together in the back seat, loose-limbed and laughing. It feels like it could be years ago, when we were both younger and less certain, but still so, so in love. It could be the night before I left for the first time, or the second time, or the fifteenth. It could be any of those early Sunday mornings, curling around each other while we tried to figure out how we could be so lucky.

But it's none of those moments. It's an interlude, a false promise, and even in the darkness my fingers find the bite mark.

He lets me kiss the bruises anyway.

Later, when Tim's a sleepy weight curled beside me, I smooth his fringe from his forehead. "What if I can't do it?" I say quietly, an admission breathed close to his ear. "What am I supposed to do without you?"

He snores softly, and doesn't give me an answer.

The moon creeps up on us. We have weeks, then days, then suddenly almost no time at all. I drive us out to the desert, out to where we can see the stars. Tim has always loved the stars.

"I've never seen them like this," he confesses, sitting on the bonnet with his back against the windshield. "There're so many."

"You city-bred witches," I tease, arm around his shoulders.

I stare at him as he examines the sky. The moonlight highlights the dusting of freckles over his nose, glinting from the whites of his eyes and the points of his teeth. I can see a bit of the wolf there, now. It makes my chest hurt.

"You know, I always thought we'd end up together," I confess, voice too thick.

"I mean, we kind of did," he says. "But just for a short time."

"I wish it was longer."

"Me, too." He sighs, turning his face into my neck. "'m tired."

"Then sleep," I advise. "I'll be here when you wake up."

He scoffs, eyes closed, and tangles our fingers together.

For a long time, I lie there and listen to him breathe. I count his freckles, stroking my thumb over the bones of his wrist. His chest rises and falls, the rest of him still in the moonlight. Slowly, carefully, I draw my gun.

I know where his heart is. I've listened to it beat for most of my life. I've heard it flutter in fear, steady in sleep, and everything in between. It's the only sound I've ever wanted to wake up to. I know where his heart is, and mine's right there along with it.

I pull the trigger.

There's noise, the kick back, and then terrible silence. No beating, no breathing; just my fingers lacing desperately with his. Still warm and slightly calloused, fingers I've loved for more than half my life.

I can smell his blood. My stomach heaves, and I keep my eyes squeezed shut. I can't look at him, don't want to remember him as anything less than alive.

My hands are steady, and the muzzle of the gun is hot where it brushes against the skin of my mouth. It burns, but it doesn't matter anymore. It's grounding, something to focus besides my own terrible heartbeat, fast and loud and all alone in the dark.

I breathe in, and I think about him appearing in my car, about empty highways in the dark and freckles on his cheekbones, about picket fences we never shared. I think about a different future.

I pull the trigger.

EJ Sidle is an Australian author who currently lives and works in Scotland. She likes stories about the supernatural, especially things with claws and teeth. Come say hi on twitter @sidle_by

To Prey

C. H. Knyght

Nell flinched as the catcalls slid over her nerves like cold slime. She curled her fingers into the strap of her bag and marched at a steady pace, refusing to let them see her scurry away like a frightened mouse. Tilting her head, Nell hid the reaction written on her face behind a veil of hair.

The vibrant rays of the sun faded as it sank behind the city horizon. Otherwise, the pack of teens might've hounded her more, but curfew close—and they weren't the reason for it. They stayed clustered on the apartment stoop, howls and whistles falling silent as she cleared the intersection. They weren't dogs; they were puppies.

Nell didn't relax until all three deadbolts slid home in the doorframe. She leaned her forehead against the door and sucked in a bracing breath. It took conscious thought to uncurl the claws of her fingers and unclench her jaw. Her teeth ached.

Safe, she was home—safe.

Someone, or something, hunted in her neighborhood. Three murders in the last couple months left everyone skittish. She'd heard their throats had been slashed open, bodies emptied of blood. Rumor had it they'd used a hatchet to almost decapitate their victims. but Nell had suspicions, that it'd been done to hide a different kind of wound, fang marks. Proven truth wasn't superstition. Nell knew in the depths of her soul the supernatural existed.

Though not the best neighborhood, it was affordable. Her minimum-wage retail job put up with her health issues and recovery days. The area also meant the cop presence wasn't heavy enough to limit the average violence. The curfew was self-enforced, fear effectively corralling them.

Her tiny blue house sat on the perimeter of a dilapidated factory lot that nature worked to reclaim. Hence the cheap price tag, a spectacular view it was not. Nell liked it. Trees pushed up through cracked concrete while vines climbed the metal stairs, covering the pitted rust with lush green.

Nell did her usual cursory scan of the bars barricading the windows. She'd need to call someone to fix the loose iron bar on the kitchen window. The rest held secure enough for now, but she'd feel better if all of them were absolutely solid. At least the silver ones held secure. Tarnished to dull gray that looked like cheap steel, those were the most important ones. Nana had told her a different sort of bedtime stories than mom, tales of the old world, so she knew silver and iron kept most supernatural beasts at bay.

Setting her groceries on the table, Nell dug out the net of garlic bulbs. She pinned the bulbs over every entrance. It wouldn't stop a vampire but it'd slow it down and be an irritation. She refused to go pleasantly with an offered arterial vein for the sucking. She'd make the night demon work for every sip if it came after her. She'd found footsteps in her flowers under the window yesterday, and smudges of mud up the side of her siding. The murderer was scoping her out.

Nightmares of blood and fangs haunted an uneasy sleep. Every odd sound made her twitch, waiting for the tap of fingernails on glass and an otherworldly request for entrance. She really hoped that part of the lore was true. She wasn't dumb enough to give it permission. The wind whispered beneath the moonlight like a mournful ghost.

Only her fanciful imagination, she knew, but her nerves twanged constantly.

In the morning, her shoulder throbbed. Nell rubbed at the phantom fangs shredding her flesh. She shivered despite the balmy summer heat. Grease from the sausages in the frying pan popped. Nell jumped. "Get ahold of yourself," she muttered.

A damp chill weighed upon the evening air. Nell tucked her head down and tried not to run from the bus stop; not that the fierce ache in her hips would let her, it was nearly that time of month. She didn't need to see the turn of the moon to know. Soon, blood would flow.

With curfew in effect, the street was desolate. A lingering customer had held her back with inane questions, and far too much information about the drama in their relationship with not one, not two, but three different guys—and they weren't poly.

And now, she was out after dark. The light of the pregnant moon edged the shadows in sharp silver like the gleam of a knife's edge. Usually, she loved the moon, but tonight something else lurked under its gaze, watching her.

Nell stopped on a corner, waiting for the walk light to change as a lone car rumbled through the intersection. The slack-faced driver paid her no attention. Three more blocks, then she'd be behind the safety of her barred windows and garlic-studded walls.

The street lamps flickered. Nell loped across the intersection as though the teeth of her nightmares nipped at her heels. Clouds blotted out the moon's guiding light. Her stride lengthened.

A hand reached out of the mouth of the alley and yanked her into the darkness between buildings. Nell yelped. Slammed against the wall, her head cracked on unyielding brick. Starbursts of pain blinded her vision.

Icy fingers clamped under her jaw, tilting her head back and forth. "Such a pretty neck you have, miss." A long thumbnail pressed against her chin, forcing her head up to expose her throat. "It looks so sweet." The smell of decay wafted over her carried by his breath.

Nell blinked tears and spots out of her vision. "Let me go," she begged.

The man's face came into focus as her sight cleared. The vampire was...pudgy and middle-aged. So much for smoldering looks and broad shoulders.

"Ah, there you are," he said and leered. He traced his tongue over the tip of a fang. Those were real enough. His gripped tightened until she wheezed, unable to draw the breath to scream.

Nell pressed against the wall, willing it to soften and allow her to sink away from his cold touch. It didn't of course. Myths made real didn't mean the laws of physics and brick were false.

His eyes glowed a dull red. "I think not. I've been watching you for a while now. Usually, I can go a month without feeding, but I couldn't wait any longer to taste you." Leaning in, he sniffed beneath her ear. Nell shuddered.

No one was coming to save her.

The moon wasn't full, not yet, but it was close to it. She could force it. The power of the silver light sang through her aching bones. It would hurt. But she wasn't prey — not tonight. The vampire would've been better off waiting a few more days, 'til after the moon's turn. He wasn't the only predator in the neighborhood — and the boys howling from their front stoops as she passed didn't qualify.

Nell called to the monster in her soul.

The wolf surged forward.

The change started with fur growing out of her skin around the bite scar on her shoulder.

The vampire hissed.

The change was agonizingly slow, every second utter torment. Nell screamed as her bones cracked. Fabric shredded and tore, stretched beyond capacity. Her skin split and sloughed to the ground like shreds of wet tissue paper as her muscles twisted around the reshaped bones. Her jawbone throbbed, and her human teeth loosened and fell out of her mouth as fangs erupted out of her bloody gums.

The vampire lurched back. "What are you?"

God, he must be new. Or extremely naïve. Did he really think he was the only existing supernatural?

Nell fell to her knees as her hips snapped and turned. Her spine arched and lengthened. Blood ran over her body in rivulets, soaking into her fur. Claws pierced out of her nail beds, peeling back her fingernails.

The crack and squelch of shifting flesh stopped. The wolf shook down, spraying blood over the vampire and alley wall.

Gathering strength, the wolf got to her hind legs and stood upright. She didn't tower, short even in this form, but she met his blood-colored gaze with a challenging stare.

"Well." The vampire scanned her new form with fascinated lust, practically drooling. "I've never tried werewolf before. I'm sure we can work around the fur."

He slunk toward her as though she was just going to stand there and wait for him to eat her.

The wolf didn't give him the warning of a growl. She lunged. He ducked, but she hadn't aimed for his throat. Unlike him, she wasn't restricted to fangs alone. The wolf plunged her fist into the vampire's chest. Curling her claws around the cold, throbbing lump of the vampire's heart, she pulled. The broken ends of his ribs gouged into her forearm. She clenched her jaw and pulled through the pain. The vampire gasped and clutched at her, grabbing fistfuls of her fur. Too late. His heartstrings snapped and she held the organ up in the moon light. Half-clotted blood stained it black.

What a disgusting creature, full of rotten, decayed meat, not even worthy being eaten. Crushing the flesh with a squelch, she sneezed at the foul scent. *Maggot.*

The wolf dropped the decayed organ onto the vampire's corpse. Movies portrayed vampires turning to dust after they were killed. Curiouser , the wolf watched, as the vampire's corpse rapidly decomposed until only viscous sludge and bone remained. Maybe it depended on the age of the vampire? The sunlight should take care of it, but not the mess from her change.

The tatters of her human skin lay on the ground like a shredded rubber mask. The wolf crouched and snuffled at the flesh before gulping it down, the shed skin would take the edge off her ravenous hunger. It took only minutes to eat it, leaving the hair and blood. Squatting over the mess, the wolf pissed. Acrid urine puddled over the ground turning pink as it mixed with the blood.

The wolf only knew that it needed to clean up, lurking in the subconscious Nell understood why. The ammonia would destroy any usable evidence. She couldn't care less what they made of the vampire's decomposed corpse as long as they couldn't tag her DNA.

The wolf loped out of the alley content and confident in the cool shadows cast by the moon. She was the top of the food chain. Even if the cops spotted her, their bullets wouldn't cause any lasting damage. Few were prepared to fight the supernatural, except other supernaturals.

Nell stretched and rolled over in the sunbeam. The mattress of moss squished beneath her as she sat up. Everything felt loose and limber as though she'd had sex, or a good hard hunt.

Nell didn't let the wolf out of the house very often. The bars on the windows weren't to keep things out, but to keep her animal half contained within. It was hard to live in the city as a were, but not impossible.

Clumps of fur scattered about her on the ground. Nell picked it up, rolling it in her fingers. From the texture, the neighborhood pride of stray cats was smaller this morning. Good, nothing too noticeable had happened then. She liked it here and she couldn't afford to move again so soon. Thankfully, the discards of her wolf fur wouldn't raise any brows even if someone stumbled over it.

Sparrows scolded her as she crawled out from under the fire escape stairs the wolf had denned under. Otherwise the factory lot was peaceful in the morning calm. Clad in nothing except sunlight, Nell padded barefoot over the cracked pavement. She didn't hurry. It was early enough—and overgrown with bushes—that she wasn't likely to be spied.

God, she needed to run more often. She felt amazing. The lingering tension headache at the base of her skull was gone, and—despite the full moon's approach—the wolf was calm, sated, instead of constantly scrabbling at her consciousness.

Sitting on the counter, clad only in an oversized shirt, Nell nursed a cup of coffee while the repairman worked on the window. He'd been remarkably prompt.

With the summer heat, he'd tied the top half of his uniform around his waist. The tank top beneath accentuated the bulge of his biceps as he bolted the bar back into place. Sweat beaded the back of his neck. Nell licked her lips, she could almost taste the salt. He had a rugged scruff to him that appealed to her appetite.

Opening the front door, Nell leaned against the frame as he packed up his tools. His strong hands were free of jewelry, silver or otherwise. *Perfect.*

"All done, ma'am," he said, flashing her an easy smile. Nell brushed her foot up the back on her calf. His eyes drifted down to her bared legs and then flicked back up as a flush darkened his ears.

"Can I offer you a cup of coffee as thanks?" Nell tilted her head, watching him through her eyelashes.

He hesitated. "I have other calls." Nell nibbled on her thumbnail, drawing his gaze to her mouth. "I really shouldn't."

Just a little nudge. Nell plucked the loose collar of her shirt and fanned it, the soft breeze swirled the hair framing her face. "It's freshly brewed, I promise, it's all hot and ready for you."

The coffee wasn't the only one.

Though calmer than normal, the wolf still lurked near the surface, and the full moon stirred her blood.

"Maybe just for a minute. The repair went quick so I have a little bit of extra time."

Nell swung the door wide and stepped back. "Come in." She licked her lips as he moved passed her inside, setting his toolbox down in the entry.

Despite the daylight hour, the sphere of the full moon peeked into the sky as the door clicked shut.

Fantasy author, C. H. Knyght enjoys expanding the known world to include a spark of wonder. Magic is what you create, make the world a better place.

Walking Dog

David J. Rank

The kid saw the cop coming long before he reached her. She remembered what Angus always told her to do when a stranger approached, "Be careful what you say."

"Hi," the cop said, turning off his flashlight. He squatted beside her in the yellow bubble of light dripping from an antiquish lamppost. He looked young, like Angus. "I'm a policeman, Officer Cuttner. What's your name?"

"Bethany." She passed a looped chain leash and collar from hand to hand, the metal links clunking tonelessly. Her bluest of eyes shifted to Cuttner's face from the darkness of the battalion of trees that marched along the path's flank. "What can I do for you … officer?"

The cop carried a radio. He touched the mike clipped to the shoulder of his black shirt. "Talking to the girl, assessing the situation."

Bethany watched him closely. She shivered—her clothes a thin windbreaker, stained, over worn sweatshirt a size too big, tattered jeans, and dirty sneakers with duct tape repairs.

"You cold?"

She was but would not admit it. "No." She wiped strings of sandy hair off her face.

"Bethany's a lovely name."

"I know." Bethany sighed and returned her attention to the woods with its nervous shadows, deeply dark, sheltered from the moon glow above. A steady breeze fomented whispers in many tongues from the foliage.

"Bethany, may I ask how old you are? Eleven? Twelve?"

She nodded.

"The park's closed."

"I know. It's quiet. I like that. Nobody around … 'cept you now."

"Why are you in the park so late, alone?"

"I'm not alone."

Cuttner stood and looked around. "Who's here with you, Bethany?"

"I was walking dog." Her voice was placid as a lobotomy.

"Where's the dog now?"

Bethany noticed his hand rested on the black gun strapped to his belt. She pointed to the dark woods. "He needed to run now so I let him."

Cuttner touched his shoulder mike and turned his head to it. "No. No backup needed. Juvenile female lost her dog. I've got it."

"Not lost."

"What?"

"Dog's not lost. Dad's out there too."

Cuttner glanced at the woods. "So you and your father were walking your dog."

Bethany slowly nodded.

"What's your father's name?"

"Angus."

"How long have you been alone, since your father left?"

She shrugged. "Not long. 'Bout since you parked your car back there." She waved a leash-free hand in the direction of the lot where Cuttner left his car.

He looked over his shoulder at the mostly dark path weaving through stout old oaks to the parking lot.

"I saw your headlights," Bethany said.

"Pets aren't supposed to run loose. You and your dad and your dog aren't supposed to be here at all this time of night."

Bethany shrugged. Her gaze never left the shadow-blotted woods. "Dog wanted to run. We like parks at night. They're quiet. We don't bother most folks."

"You and your father live near here?"

"Nope."

"Where do you live? Can you tell me, Bethany?"

She focused on him again. "Our car, mostly." She pointed in the direction of a not so near street. "Campgrounds sometimes, waysides. We move a lot. Dad don't like to be in any one place too long. Staying put's not good for you, he says. Gotta see the world."

"You and your dad have a last name, Bethany?"

She stared into the shrouded woods. "Not really. Dad says it ain't nobody's business but ours. Angus and Bethany is enough."

"Where's your mother?"

"Dead. Long time now."

"I'm sorry."

She shrugged.

Cuttner aimed his flashlight into the woods. "Your dad's in those trees."

Bethany nodded.

"He left you here to chase after the dog."

She hesitated, and nodded.

Cuttner peered into the woods, saw only vertical lines in patchy darkness, heard only the chatter of wind-motivated leaves. He didn't speak for a long moment.

Thinking about things, Bethany decided. She watched as his hand hovered above the radio mike clipped to his blue shirt. She was relieved when he lowered his arm.

A branch snapped.

"Angus? This is the police, Officer Cuttner. I'm with your daughter. She's okay but we need to talk, Angus."

Movement rippled within the shadow-stained darkness. Something heavy loped through the underbrush.

A growl—low and gurgly. The cop's body tightened. Bethany did not react.

"What's your dog's name?" He popped open the strap securing his gun in its holster while he scanned the trees with the flashlight.

"Dog, just dog. Dad don't want to give him no other name. Says he don't deserve it."

Another growl, this time deep-throated, primeval. Cuttner's fingers curled around his gun's grip.

"How big is your dog, Bethany?"

"Big."

"Big enough it could hurt people?"

She shrugged. "Dad's with him."

"I'm not so sure about that." Cuttner stepped closer to the woods. "Angus? If you hear me, respond please. I just want to know you're all right. Your daughter's worried about you." He glanced at Bethany.

She yawned.

"Angus, do you have control of your dog? Do you need assistance? Are you injured?"

Something shuffled in the leaf litter buried in the night a dozen or so yards ahead of him.

"Angus?" A heartbeat later Cuttner turned to Bethany. "You stay there, right there in the light. Understand? Don't move."

She nodded, the leash gripped in both hands.

"I'll be back—with your father."

Cuttner pointed the flashlight ahead of him and followed the beam through brush into the woods.

"Angus, I'm coming to help you subdue your dog. If you don't need my help come out now where I can see you. Angus?"

Cuttner did not wait for an answer. Pulling out his gun, he stepped deeper into the woods away from the lamplight.

Humming softly, Bethany saw the glow of his flashlight here and there. The cop called out once … twice. She heard a grunt ended with a garbled cough and a gurgle cut short like a severed hose. In the dark a heavy thing crashed into the leaf litter. Dog growled. It would not be rabbits or deer or some stray pet that satiated him tonight. Things ripped, other things snapped. Dog was such a messy eater.

Bethany waited. She knew what she'd soon have to do. When he was done, dog would return to her and Bethany would slip the collar around his neck and lead him back to the car. She'd have to drive again tonight. Bethany didn't care for that but they'd have to leave quickly. No waiting for daylight this time. She'd drive out of town while dog slept, and find a quiet place to stop miles from here, someplace where Bethany could get clean water to wash the blood off dog like she always did.

And come daybreak, when Angus returned, he'd toast bread for her over an open fire and she'd slather peanut butter on the toast with sliced banana and she'd eat while Angus would stare into the fire and weep. He'd feel bad for a day or so.

Bethany loved the smell of a campfire. She loved toasted peanut butter and banana sandwiches in the morning. The thought made her smile.

She loved her dad and he loved her back. Everything would be fine now for another month.

After breakfast, she'd sleep the rest of the day in the back seat as Angus drove them far, far from this park. To another pretty place … maybe Oregon this time.

David J. Rank is a published author, editor, recovering journalist, founder and director of the nonprofit Novel-In-Progress Bookcamp & Writing Retreat educational programs

since 2014. His more than 30 dark fiction short stories have been published in regional literary publications, various online magazines, and three anthologies.

He is a supporting member of the Horror Writers Association, organizing the HWA-Wisconsin Chapter in 2018. A member of both Wisconsin Writers Association and Chicago Writers Association, he was president of the WWA from 2013 to 2016.

Werewolf Eulogy

Adam Stemple

Fall scoots out of Minnesota as fast as the migrating ducks. Not the mallards—pond pigeons, I call them—they stick around. Don't know how they make it through the thirty below weather, but there's always still plenty of them come spring. But the other ducks—wood ducks, buffleheads, teal, mergansers—they scamper out of the state at the first sign of snow.

They know what's coming.

People don't share that instinct. We're like the dumb ducks of the waterfowl world.My old man used to say about certain people, "They don't have the sense that God gave geese." People round here don't even have that. Geese know when it's time to make a vee and head south.

Not that I'm bragging. Just this morning I was digging through my closet, pulling out my down jacket and my pilot's hat lined with Russian rabbit fur. You wouldn't think a Norwegian would buy anything Russian, but they know from cold. And that's not even enough. I got flannel to go under the coat. Wool socks and long johns. Insulated boots. Two pairs of gloves that I wear at the same time. And a thermal face mask.

That's right, it's so cold your face freezes off if you leave it uncovered. Ridiculous place, Minnesota, but dumb ducks that we are, we love it.

Now, I explain this to you so when I tell you about the werewolf raiding my chicken house, you don't ask a lot of silly questions like "Why didn't you leave?"

I'm Minnesotan. The air kills you here. If that don't scare you off, what will?

I remember it was the height of summer when I first saw the werewolf. Didn't know what it was then, of course, but I knew it was something weird. You'd think what with it being so cold in the winter, summers in Minnesota would be mild. But no, the summers are as brutal as the winters, with hundred degree days, thousand percent humidity, and ten thousand lakes—which means ten thousand mosquito breeding areas.

We like to joke and say the mosquito's our state bird, but we're not really kidding.

So with it being so hot, I wasn't sleeping so good. I'd got up out of bed and was in the kitchen making myself a midnight snack when I heard a ruckus coming from outside.

Something's found the chickens, I thought. *I hope it's not a weasel.*

Everything out in the woods will eat a chicken. Especially the Cornish Crosses that I raise. They're basically a feathered hamburger, only dumber. But only a weasel will slaughter the whole flock and paint the walls of the chicken house with their blood.

I grabbed a shovel instead of my shotgun. Didn't want to fire a load of buckshot in there and do the weasel's work for him. Besides, I've found waving a shovel and shouting like a crazy person will scare off most anything, even bears. Once I knew what was attacking the chickens I'd find the right tool to deal with it, whether it was poison, trap, or bullet.

So, I ran out into my backyard. The motion sensors had turned on the flood lights and I saw that the top of my chicken house was torn clean off. Leaning into it was some kind of beast, but with most of its torso inside, I couldn't tell what it was. Just two big legs covered in dark fur, feet on the ends of them long like a man's but clawed like an animal, bushy tail pointing straight up and wagging a little like an excited dog.

Then it stood up. Thing was nearly seven feet tall. It had a chicken in each hand—because that's what they were, despite being tipped with long claws. Big furry head like a giant bullet and teeth so big that a bunch of them overlapped its lower lip. Bit of gray around the muzzle. Its torso was covered in the same dark fur as its legs and head, though thinner on its belly, which rippled with ab muscles like a pro athlete's, despite the eight sagging dugs that hung in two rows.

Well, I thought, *whatever it is, it's a female.*

As I watched, the she-beast bit the head off the chicken in her left hand. The chicken, true to its nature, kept struggling. The beast's tail, true to its nature as well, was definitely wagging now.

"Hey there!" I shouted. "Lay off them chickens!"

She turned my way then, and I could see her eyes, gold like a wolf's.

Maybe not your best plan there, I said to myself. Way too late, if you ask me.

The beast roared and I swear it shook the ground. But I don't scare easy, specially not in my own backyard, and I roared right back at her and waved my shovel in the air.

Hey, it works on the bears. And this thing was big, but it wasn't six-hundred pound bruin big. It probably went about three-twenty, three-forty, and like I said, was near seven feet tall. I'm not *huge* for a Minnesotan, but I'm still north of six feet if my disc isn't acting up. And back then I carried more weight in my shoulders than my belly, if you know what I mean. If it came down to it, the beast probably liked her chances more than mine, but a good clout to the head with a shovel can change opinions in a hurry.

It looked like she was sizing me up, thinking about it. So I took a step forward and shouted louder. It doesn't do to let big animals know you're afraid of them. Usually makes them more aggressive, not less. Meanwhile, I was thinking that was as far as I'd go and if the thing charged me I could still make it to the house at a run. But me advancing seemed to decide her and she turned, leapt over the fencing easily, and loped off into the woods, still holding two of my chickens.

"Aw, geez," I muttered, afraid to look in the chicken house and see how many I'd lost.

I wanted nothing more than to go back in the house and crack open that new bottle of Windsor and take as many slugs as I needed to make this night go away, but there was a chicken roof needed mending, not to mention a bunch of blood making the roofless chickens more nervous than they already were. So instead of a stiff drink and a soft bed, I put the chickens in the mud room and stayed up half the night cleaning and repairing. By the time I was done and had the survivors tucked back into their home, I was too tired to do anything but slink back inside and go to sleep.

I slept late the next day, which is a privilege a lot of us retired guys have earned but rarely take advantage of, me being no exception. But I figured I'd earned myself some rest, what with chasing off the whatever it was the night before. So I stayed in bed till it was nearly eight in the morning, then got up to make coffee and call the DNR.

"Department of Natural Resources. How can I help you?"

You can stop trying to give me tickets for hunting on my own land, I thought but didn't say anything. I've never found a situation where staying quiet and not saying the first thing that pops into your head *wasn't* a good idea.

"Oh ya, um, hi there," I said. I've never been great on the phone. Hard to gauge how your words are landing when you can't see the face of the fella you're talking to.

"How can I help you, sir?"

At least the girl on the phone was polite. Sometimes the people working the phones at these places are…well, it wouldn't be nice to say. But polite isn't the word I'd use.

"I chased a creature out of my chicken house last night. Big thing. Thought you guys ought to know about it."

"Do you know what kind of animal it was?"

"Didn't say it was an animal. If it was an animal, I woulda said so. It was a creature."

"Um…yes sir. What did this *creature* look like?"

I described the thing to her and she didn't say anything for a short while. When she spoke again, she didn't sound polite anymore.

"You know, sir, we do a tough job here at the DNR. An important job. And well, wasting our time telling us a *werewolf* is tearing up your chicken house…well, geez, it's not very nice."

When a phone conversation gets that ugly that quickly there's nothing to do but say goodbye. So I did. And that was that for the DNR. At least now I had a name for the creature that had killed my chickens.

Werewolf.

You might think an old widower living by himself up north wouldn't know much about computers. Well, you'd be right. But my youngest set me up with internet a while ago and I know how to google. So, a couple hours after talking to the rude girl at the DNR, I knew all about werewolves. Most importantly, I knew I'd need silver bullets to kill one. Which I also knew I could get. I wasn't one of those hunters who made his own bullets, but you spend any time at the diner during deer season or at the range any season at all and you're going to meet some guys who do. I'm sure I could melt down one of my wife's old candlesticks or something like that. Have one of those gun-crazy fellas make me some silver bullets. I was a fair shot, and the werewolf was a big target; I didn't see how it would be any kind of problem to kill it. Thing was, there was something else important the Google told me about werewolves.

They were people.

Well, most of the time they were people. And while I've got no trouble killing something I'm going to eat, I sure enough draw the line at killing people. I had two kids in the service and both saw active duty. And even though they came back unharmed, they didn't come back whole, if you know what I mean. Killing another human being takes something from you, and I'm not sure you ever get it back.

But then again, what kind of man can't protect the animals under his care? It was a pickle, sure enough, and a sour one at that.

But, I thought, *at least I don't have to worry until the moon is full again.*

And maybe not even then. There was no guarantee I'd ever see the beast again. Maybe it was just passing through. And I'm not much given to worry, anyway. Preparation, sure. I reinforced the chicken shed and put a stronger, taller fence around it. Put in big bolt locks on the doors of my house and boarded up the ground floor windows. Made sure my shotgun was all cleaned and oiled.

Just cause I didn't want to kill the thing didn't mean I wouldn't put a load of buckshot in its chest to discourage it from beheading any more chickens.

I laid in bandages and antiseptic and bolstered my supply of ibuprofen. Gassed up the truck in case I had to take the long trip to the hospital in the city. And I read everything I could about werewolves.

So, I was feeling pretty prepared as I sat on my porch during the next full moon, though I can't pretend that the thought of facing down a deathless, cursed beast didn't give me at least a little pause. But I always say, no matter what comes, you gotta put your boots on and do your chores. 'Cause don't you know in all my years, I've never yet seen them do themselves.

So do your worst, she-wolf, I thought as I sat in the dark and waited. *I won't hide or run away.*

I didn't have to wait long.

The sun was barely down and the moon barely up when she slunk soundlessly into my yard. The new fence didn't prove much of an obstacle; she sliced through the corrugated steel like it was Wisconsin cheddar. Punching through the chicken house roof, she peeled it back like she was opening an old can of Hamm's. By this time I was off my porch, shotgun in hand. Firing into the air, I shouted at her. It'd worked last time, I didn't see why it wouldn't work again.

It didn't.

Maybe she'd spent her month preparing, as well, because she wasn't put off by loud noises this time. Before the shotgun blast even stopped echoing, she shed the roof from her claw and rushed me.

In the old days, I would have had an over-under and been cursing myself for putting one of my two available shells into the air. But these new guns have room for more ammo than you ever have ducks to shoot at, so I got off three blasts before turning and running for my door. I hit with every one—like I said, I'm a fair shot and she's a big target—and they definitely stung her. But they sure didn't slow her down much.

She caught the back of my leg just as I stepped inside. Claws that could shear through corrugated steel weren't slowed much by the denim of my jeans and they sawed four long gashes down my calf. But I didn't fall and managed to both escape into the house and slam the door shut in her face. The impact of her running into the door shook the whole house, but it was three inches of solid oak. It'd take a bomb to knock that door down.

Of course, it hadn't been tested against werewolf claws. She gave the door a couple of swipes and it sounded like they dug in deep. Real deep. I didn't figure it'd take more than a couple minutes for her to shred the door so much that she could step through it like one of those old beaded curtains. But I guess werewolves aren't patient critters, because she stopped when the door didn't give up the ghost immediately like the chicken house roof had. Or maybe she was more interested in keeping me out of the way while she ate, because instead of looking for another way in she went right back to the chicken house. I could tell by the screams of the dying birds.

That hurt. But there was nothing I could do. If I went back out there, she'd just chase me back inside again. And with my leg all tore up, she might catch me this time. Even if I did make it back in, she'd for sure claw the door up a couple more times. If I gave her too many chances at that, she was going to get in. The door wouldn't stop her. The boarded over windows wouldn't stop her. My guns wouldn't stop her. All that was left was to hunker down and live through the night. Figure out a new plan in the morning.

Maybe one that involves a silver bullet this time?

I was feeling a bit of a fool for not having at least one of those in reserve. But still, I'd been in scrapes before and gotten out of them without killing anyone. Seemed like a silly habit to pick up this late in life.

Well, it was a long night and no lie. The werewolf tore through the chickens while I bandaged my leg up nice and tight. Then she snuffled around the house for a bit. I didn't hear anything more from her after that, but didn't dare go out to see if she'd gone. Didn't dare doze off, either, so I was dead tired when dawn finally came and I went out and surveyed the damage.

It was pretty bad. The chickens were a total loss. And though the chicken house looked repairable, with no chickens, why bother? Sure, I could get more, raise them up again. But my heart wasn't in it. If I couldn't protect them, there was no sense having them. And yeah, I was going to eat them myself eventually, but there's a difference. Can't say exactly what it is, but it's definitely there.

Good news was, with no more chickens, I figured I wouldn't have to worry about the werewolf anymore. I gave a long sigh and set to work tearing down the ruined chicken house. But I had trouble concentrating. And it wasn't just how tired I was. It was that the thought of not seeing the werewolf again bothered me.

Me and her have some unfinished business, I thought. And though she clearly had the upper hand in wolf form, if we met while she was human, I thought things might go a bit differently. *Maybe a lot differently.*

Of course, there was the small problem of finding her. I wasn't any kind of tracker, but I thought, *How hard can it be? I sure won't confuse her tracks for anything else. Plus she's huge and probably dripping buckets of chicken blood.*

I put my tools back in the garage and grabbed a quick breakfast. Changed the bandage on my leg. I was dead tired, but this needed to be done before any kind of summer storm came through and swept the tracks away.

Why waste your life sleeping? I thought. *The grave is a fine and quiet place, and a perfect place for rest.*

I started at the chicken house and yeah, she was a messy eater. Bloody tracks lead northwest out of the yard. I limped after them. The trail was easy to follow for a time: big muddy footprints, broken branches on underbrush, blood spatter from the murdered chickens. When the chickens were all eaten, it got a little tougher, but by then I knew what I was looking for. I tracked her for hours, deep into the boggy woods, over thin streams, through shallow gullies, and up into the low hills. I was miles from my home, now, and not sure if I'd make it back before dark. Also, between the lack of sleep and my aching calf, I was just about dead on my feet.

Then I lost the trail.

"Darn it all," I said out loud. I searched in expanding circles from where I'd last seen any sign, even getting on my knees in spots. But even nose to the ground I couldn't find any clue as to where the werewolf might have gone.

But as I creaked to my feet, I finally lifted my eyes from the forest floor and noticed something I hadn't seen before: a clearing a hundred yards out with a small cabin in it.

"Well, would you look at that?" I whispered.

Hunkered down in the bushes, I examined the cabin. It was a tiny place, five or six hundred square feet total, just the one level, like a "little place up north" people in the cities buy and then visit maybe once every few years. But it looked like it was well kept, the tiny yard trimmed, little garden clear of weeds. Nobody went in or out for the half-hour I watched. I would've watched for longer, but I was in danger of falling asleep in the woods. And with a werewolf running around, that didn't seem like the safest thing to do.

Nothing for it but to do it, I thought, and marched up to the front door. Knocked sharply. Just before the door opened, I saw lying in the perfect grass to the left of the door what had been hidden from my view by a slight rise in the lawn: a single decapitated chicken. But it was too late to change course because just then the door opened and I was looking down at a woman in a bathrobe, her hair still wet from showering. She was older, like me, but had dyed half of her silver hair a metallic yet somehow still muted blue. She was tall—maybe five-ten or so— and muscled lean like a distance runner. And she had eyes the same golden color as the wolf's.

"Yes?" she said, her accent making me think of tall mountains and deep forests in Eastern European countries I didn't know the name of.

"Oh ya, um, hi there," I said. I'm not so great talking to women.

She looked me up and down then, taking in my unshaven face, my rumpled clothes, the shredded and bloodstained leg of my jeans. And, of course, the shotgun I carried.

"Oh God," she said, "were those your chickens? I am *so* sorry!"

Then she stepped back and waved me inside.

I don't know why I went in. Clearly she was the werewolf that had nearly killed me the night before. She probably just wanted to finish the job in private. But she seemed honestly heartbroken over the chickens, and she was just so nice, and well, I hadn't had a woman look me up and down like that since my wife died twelve years earlier. So maybe if you're a lonely old man who lives by himself out in the woods and doesn't do much but chop wood, talk to his kids a couple times a month, and read the same six books over and over, then the risk of violent death might be worth it to spend a little time talking to a great gal like Joan.

Now, I know that's not her real name, but I never could wrap my mouth around those syllables, so she told me it was okay to call her that.

We spent that whole day drinking coffee and talking and finding out we were two peas in a pod. We were both independent, didn't need anything from anybody. Grew our own food, raised or hunted our own meat. Neither of us liked living around other people. Her because she might kill them, and me, well, just because. We liked the same music: old country. It was just that the countries were different.

We laughed over that a lot, so same sense of humor.

And though we both loved our families, we didn't feel the need to see them all the time. Holidays and special occasions was fine.

When night fell she didn't turn into a wolf.

"It's just the one night a month," she assured me.

Instead, she gave me a ride home in her little Prius, which I was surprised she would drive way out where we lived, what with the winters we get. But she loved the gas mileage and liked that it was better for the environment, and turns out it was actually good in the snow, though I did have to haul it out of the woods with the truck in that big storm we got in December of twenty-twelve.

Anyway, the next day I went out to see her again, but first I drove two hours south to the nearest grocery store and bought some chicken. First time I'd *bought* chicken in probably thirty years. Got a bottle of wine, too, though I didn't know if it was any good. We cooked the chicken on a grill in her backyard and drank the wine—it tasted like flat grape pop to me but she said it was a "fine vintage"— and when the stars came out she told me how they looked through a wolf's eyes.

We had twenty good years together, Joan and I. And though I know that's a tenth of what some of you had with her, we still packed a lot into those years. I always figured I'd go first, what with being mortal and all. But forget lycanthropy, cancer is the real curse. She faced it, of course, with the fierce animal intensity that she took into any battle. And even though it eventually killed her, it never beat her. She went out snarling defiance to the very end.

Which, I guess, is how we all want to go. It's like that old Irish poet said, but instead of raging against the dying of the light, she raged against the dying of the night. Because though she sometimes complained about that one night a month, worried as she was about hurting people or their pets, I knew she wouldn't give it up for nothing. She reveled in the freedom of it, the wildness.

I never asked her to give it up. Never searched for a cure. Never did anything more than hide myself away during the full moon so she wouldn't kill me. She'd have felt real bad about that, don't you know.

But I did build her a chicken house of her very own. One with a hinged roof, so I wouldn't have to replace it every month. Because, oh boy, did she like eating them chickens.

Adam Stemple is an award-winning author, poet, and musician who lives in the frozen wasteland that is Minnesota.

The Big L

Richard Pulfer

Twenty-nine days without incident, I wrote upon the calendar before circling the date. The pungent odor of the red marker drifted off the glossy paper. If I stood much closer, the room would start spinning. I ignored the cute kittens on the cover. Diana had given it to me as a home-warming present.

As if this place could ever be my home.

On the surface, Forest Ridge wasn't that bad. I had visited war buddies in retirement homes that smelt like piss and prune juice. Compared to those shitholes, Forest Ridge was almost heaven. *Almost*.

Beyond my door, I could hear the orderlies marching from room to room with military precision. Cameras sat perched in every hallway corner. I didn't need twenty years in the Chicago PD to know that something was rotten about Forest Ridge.

"Yo gramps," a deep voice rang out from behind my door. "You decent?"

"No, Matthews. I'm buck-naked. Enter at the risk of feeling extremely inadequate," I announced. The door sounded like a bank vault as it swung aside with a dense metallic squeal. Matthews gave a baritone chuckle as he entered the room, though not before ensuring I was indeed fully clothed. I could smell his cheap, musky cologne.

"Jackass," Jerome Matthews grunted as he pulled in a tray of food.

The chief orderly towered at six foot six, with shoulders as wide as barbells and just as hard. Deep black marks run from his shoulder down to his forearm, half from a fading Semper Fidelis tattoo and the rest from where IED shrapnel had cut into him in Afghanistan.

I liked Matthews. We were both Bears fans and both jarheads. The guy carried himself like a linebacker stepping through a minefield. Which begged the question: how did Matthews go from dodging RPG's in Afghanistan to cleaning sheets in Forest Ridge?

Don't get paranoid, I reminded myself, *otherwise they'll never let you go. Get healthy and get the hell out.*

"Are the amenities to your liking?" Matthews asked. "We took the liberty of bolting everything down twice in case you have another incident."

"They're fine," I said as I ran my hands over the smooth, warm sheets. The refreshing odor of fabric softener permeated my nostrils. "If I'd known all I had to do to get rock star treatment was trash, I'd have tossed my TV into the swimming pool on the first night."

"Yeah, well, your night terrors are getting expensive," Matthews said. "At least that's what the doc says."

"Siodmak can kiss my wrinkly blue ass," I replied.

"I know, I know," Matthews sighed. "You sure you don't want a sedative for tonight? It will knock you right out."

"I'm sure," I replied. *If I start popping pills now, it'll give them one more reason to keep me here. I gotta stay sharp, stay focused.*

Stay me.

"Well, let me know if you need anything," Matthews said. He deposited the warm plate of food on a small fold-out table before he pushed his cart out of the room. "Or if you change your mind about those pills."

"Thanks, but I'll be fine," I said.

There were really only two things to do in Forest Ridge: the boob tube or bingo, but neither appealed to me. The volume knob was broken on the TV, loudly blaring "The Price is Right" like a Led Zeppelin concert. I decided to turn in for the night.

Even without bingo or the tube, my sleep was interrupted. Matthews' booming voice echoed through the halls, but it was Doctor Siodmak's soft, withered voice that made my fists tighten.

"The man is a stubborn pain in the ass!" Siodmak snarled. I was glad the feeling was mutual.

"He's just adjusting," Matthews said.

"Have you seen the bill for the room yet?" I heard Sidomak grumble. "All of that stuff is specially-made, you know."

What exactly was specially-made? The room consisted of mostly a small LED HDTV on a stand across from the lumpy hospital bed and an ottoman.

More like cheaply made.

"If it were up to me, he'd be in the isolation ward," Siodmak said. What kind of nursing home had an isolation ward?

"You know he's not that bad," Matthews said in a calmer voice. "He just needs more time."

"Has he mentioned anything else about the accident?" Siodmak's voice almost softened to a whisper.

The car accident was the go-to subject for everyone trying to keep me in rehab. I told them what I told the cops: there was something in the road. I swerved, ran headlong into an oak tree. I did my time in rehab and now I wanted out. For some reason, the play-by-play just wasn't floating their boats. Maybe their quota for curmudgeons was low or something.

"Just the usual . . . he swerved, hit a tree, the usual song-and-dance," Matthews said on the other side of the door. I don't consider ramming into an oak tree at forty-five miles per hour a "song and dance".

"Perhaps we need to consider alternate treatments," Siodmak said. "It's your call as head of security,"

"Meaning if it blows up in my face," Matthews said. "It's on me."

After a beat, Siodmak said, "Just think about it."

I backed away from the door, returning to my bed and tossing the blankets over my head. I know I wouldn't sleep. So instead I spent the next few hours gazing at the ceiling.

I thought I'd lost my Alice years ago, but I saw her in my daughter Diana every day. With two divorces and four kids, life had not been kind to my little girl. She was the reason I needed to get out.

"And you sure you haven't met anyone else at work?" I said, watching as the sun cuts kaleidoscope shapes through the line of leafy maple trees.

"No, I think I'm done with men for a while," Diana said.

"Okay, how about women then?" I replied with a grin.

"No, Dad, no!" Diana said with mock indignation. "What about you?"

"Hmmm," I said, distracted by a familiar clicking sounds.

"Making eyes at any foxy ladies at the bingo table?" she asked with a mischievous smile.

"What? No!" I said. "I think it's a little late for me to get back into the dating scene."

"If I can do it after two marriages, you can definitely do it after just one. We'll be each other's wingman," she replied. "Deal?"

I could never tell when she was being serious about things like this. I nodded towards a small park bench in the shade, barely touched by the cool morning dew. The grass tickled the top of my heels as I moved towards the park bench. Diana was already on her smartphone.

"Deal," I answered with a gruff sigh.

I could hear a familiar clicking noise from behind the nearby bushes. I asked Matthews about it once, and he told me it was probably just the sprinkler systems, but I knew the sound of camera when I heard one. There were cameras everywhere in this place –- in the halls, the cafeteria, probably even in my room.

"Dad--" Diana asked, her eyes looking up from her phone. She sets down the phone next to her on the bench. "Is everything alright?"

"Sorry," I said. "I must have dozed off."

I caught the familiar scent of cheap cologne in the air. Matthews must have been somewhere nearby.

"If you want to talk about your night terrors . . . I'm here, you know?" Diana said in a slow, plodding voice. I could tell she was treading carefully.

"I'm fine, honey. No incidents for the last twenty-nine days," I grinned.

Diana gave me the same look Alice used to give me when I tried to pull a fast one. "And what about the night terrors?"

I gave her my best sheepish smile and replied, "Well, I haven't been sleep-walking at all."

"I know, Dad. And that's great. But a month after the accident, you just up and disappeared," Diana said. "The next morning the cops found you walking along the side of the road. I was worried out of my mind. I can't go through that again."

"That's why you have to stay here. Until we know everything is . . . okay," Diana said softly.

I nodded, if only to indicate I had heard her.

"But if you ever do need to talk to anyone about something, you know I'm here, right?" she kept pressing. I took her hand and gave it a warm squeeze.

"I do know that, honey," I said. "But you have to see I'm okay. I survived cancer, a heart attack and your mom's terrible cooking."

Diana turned away, if only to hide the laugh spreading across her face. "She burnt everything she ever put in the oven. She could barely manage a microwave dinner."

She faced me once more, her skin paled. "I miss her so much."

"I know you do, honey. I do too," I said, keeping her hand in mine. "But I'm not going anywhere. This is just a speed bump in the road to recovery."

Diana returned the sheepish look, turning away for a brief moment. "Speaking of speed bumps," she said. "Do you remember anything about the accident?"

I could feel my expression darkening, my face contorting as my skin flustered with both embarrassment and anger. I jerked my hand out of Diana's reach. I looked away, focusing the catacomb of trees directly ahead.

"I told everyone what happened," I said. "That's still not good enough, is it?"

"Dad, that's not it," Diana started.

"Then why do you keep asking about it?" I raised my voice. "What do you think it's going to change?"

Diana's lips trembled as she searches my face for any sign of comfort. She found none, so when her phone starts to beep a minute later, she simply said, "I need to take this."

"You do that," I replied briskly as I stood up.

"Dad, I--" Diana started, but it was too late. I was already halfway down the path.

Sometimes you're a real dick, Frank, I told myself.

Matthews was waiting for me in my room. His big arms crossed his chest as he regarded me with a surly expression. I sighed, knowing what this is about.

"You change your mind about that sedative?" he asked.

"I doubt there's a pill that can fix all the things going through my head right now," I said.

"What if I told you there was?" he replied.

Well, things just got interesting.

"Excuse me?" I asked.

"Well, it's not actually a pill," Matthews shrugged. "It's a treatment."

I took a seat on my bed and gestured for Matthews to do the same. "Just what all does this mysterious treatment involve?" I asked.

"You ever been hypnotized before?" he replied. I immediately laughed.

"You've got to be kidding me," I said. I always regarded hypnotists as little more than con artists and phone-in psychics. I busted both on the streets of Chicago.

"I'll take that as a 'no'," Matthews said with a smirk.

"I don't even know if I can be hypnotized," I admitted.

"Yeah, nearly everyone who hasn't been hypnotized says that. Don't worry. The doc is very good at it," Matthews said.

"The doctor . . . you mean Siodmak?" I raised an eyebrow.

Matthew nodded slowly.

This time I had just enough presence of mind not to smirk or chuckle. Hypnosis was just the kind of second-rate bullshit I'd expected Siodmak to peddle. Not that I told Matthews any of that.

"So, it's just hypnosis?" I asked.

"Mostly, yes," Matthews answered. "It's a possible way of determining what's causing these night terrors and how they can be prevented in the future."

"And it's painless?" I said.

"Physically, it should be," Matthews said.

"What do you mean, should be?" I shot back.

"In rare cases, the process can be physically painful," Matthews replied.

"What about mentally?" I asked.

"Well, that's a question for the doctor to answer," Matthews said. "But the treatment isn't without risks."

He leaned forward as he spoke. I looked him straight in the eye. Matthews trusted the Doc on this, and I trusted Matthews. He might have been playing his cards close to the chest, but he hadn't steered me wrong yet.

"Will it get me the hell out of this place?" I asked. At first, Matthews was quiet. He finally answered.

"It will improve your condition," he said.

I wanted out. I wanted my life back. If my condition improved, whatever that might be, this treatment might be the only way out of this place.

"Don't you need my daughter's say-so on this?" I asked. "I mean, she does have the power of attorney."

"She already agreed," Matthews said.

I feel my rage, but this time I managed to keep my temper in check. I hated being left out of the loop. Like it or not, my back was against the wall.

"Okay, I'm in," I finally said. "When is the procedure?"

"Tonight," Matthews said, standing up and heading for the door. "We're running out of time."

You're telling me. There wasn't a single window in my room, but I could feel the night falling fast. The hair on my neck started to rise.

Hours later, two orderlies knocked on my door. Matthews wasn't among them. They loaded me onto a squeaky wheelchair and pushed me down the hallway.

One orderly -- a stocky young man -- steered the wheelchair as quickly as a shopper in the middle of a Black Friday sale. The other man bristled with caution whenever we approached a corner.

Another veteran.

He wasn't the only one. When the stocky man reached forward to the elevator button, I could see a tattoo on his arm, probably Ranger or Airborne. I wondered why this place employed so many veterans.

The two men ushered me into a small room. The walls and floor were completely white. *This doesn't look promising. This looks like a loony bin.* The only break in the whiteness was a large horizontal mirror to my right. *Is this a padded cell or an interrogation room?* They wheeled me to the solitary object in the room – a dentist chair.

As if they couldn't get freaky enough? What are they going to do now? Drill a root canal?

With some trepidation, I hoisted myself into the plush light blue leather of the dentist chair. I laid back into a reclined position. I doubt there was a person alive who could relax in one of those contraptions. I rested on the plush leather of the chair as the two orderlies strap me in.

"Usually I ask for someone to buy me a drink before they tie me up like this," I said. "I'm old-fashioned that way."

"Frank," I heard Siodmak's voice crackling through an intercom behind me. "Are you ready to begin?"

"Sure, doc," I said. "Just don't make me do anything stupid when I'm out."

Siodmak didn't respond. Instead, the two orderlies gave me a somewhat reassuring nod and walked out of the room. Instead, the gentle sound of rolling waves filled the room with a slight hiss of sand being pushed by the incoming tide. I laid my head back and try to relax.

"You sure you don't want to light some candles for the mood?" I said.

"Just concentrate, Frank," Siodmak says. "That's all I ask."

Siodmak didn't inspire much confidence. My heart started to slow, but something else was relaxing me. I heard the background noise through the intercom, as the sound of waves continued to stretch across the shore. A large gray light lured me in closer and closer. Eventually, weariness weighs down my eyelids until there is nothing but blackness.

"Frank . . . " Siodmak said, but it was not his voice that I heard, but my own.

. . . tell me about the car accident.

Frank was driving home from visiting his wife's grave on their anniversary. He left the cemetery just before nightfall. Then Frank saw something in the road.

Where was this?

Along Route 2.

What did you do when you saw it in the road?

Frank noticed it was still twitching. He thought it was an animal that had been struck by a car. Poor thing. He swerved to miss it.

Did you lose control of the car then?

No.

When did you lose control of the car?

Frank saw it was still alive. It darted towards the car just as he was passing it. He jerked the wheel to the left, causing the car to bounce through the ditch. Frank's car plowed into a nearby tree.

The thing in the road, was it an animal?

Yes.

Are you sure?

No.

Was it dead?

No.

What happened next?

The thing bolted towards Frank. He thought it had to be injured since it ran on two legs instead of four. The passenger side window exploded into shards of glass. That's how it got Frank.

What happened next?

Its large toothy snout burst through the window, clamping down on Frank's arm like a vice grip. Pain shot through Frank's arm. With his free hand, Frank thumped it with an ice-scrapper. The thing released Frank's throbbing hand from its grip. For a brief moment, night became day as piercing high-beams of another car streaked down the road. In the newfound light, Frank saw the thing in full —

A loud click broke through the haze. I knew it was the sound of a rifle being loaded. I started to fight against my bonds.

We're losing him.

I turned to the two-way mirror pleading for help. I expected to find solace in my reflection. Instead I saw the thing . . . the thing from that night . . . the thing that had been in the road starring back at me with its black, yellow-rimed eyes. It drew back its mouth to reveal rows of sharp teeth.

It tore through the bounds which once kept it flat against the soft slab. The stench of man filled this place. It was anxious to leave. Its ear twitched as a series of clicks sounded behind it, followed by a musky smell.

It twisted around to face its attackers. There are three of them, all holding long metallic shapes in their hands. With no other option, it charged at the men. Several long, sharp objects poked into its long, furry hide, as a solitary word clawed from somewhere deep within its mind.

Poison.

It dropped to its knees, its elbows following suit. The world spun around its eyes. Soon it was greeted only by the darkness and the silence.

I couldn't remember waking up. My consciousness simply turned on, as if a light switch had been flipped. I was sitting in an office, my ass now planted in a wheelchair. Siodmak stood in front of me.

"That's why Matthews recommended the sedatives. It's a lot less jarring to wake up from an episode like a bad dream, instead of simply . . . being," Siodmak said, sitting on the ottoman next to my bed.

"I'm not going home, am I?" I asked. Siodmak gave me another weak smile and then shook his head.

"That was all me last night, wasn't it? You had to put me down, in the end," I said.

"With tranquilizers. Had you breached those doors Matthews would have put you down for good. One of his men was loading a rifle on the other side of the door for that purpose. We believe the sound brought you out of the trance prematurely," Siodmak said. "Had you escaped you would have been a danger to everyone."

"Which is why I can't go home," I said. "So just what is it? Some of kind of schizophrenia?"

Siodmak didn't answer. Instead, he reached for a book on his shelf, opened to a bookmarked page, and handed me the heavy volume. I look downed to see a heavily-underlined segment in the midst of several other definitions.

Lycanthropy: The reoccurring metamorphosis from the form of man to the form of wolf, or somewhere in between.

"You've got to me kidding me," I said.

"Think about the symptoms. Your senses are extraordinarily sharp," Siodmak looked me straight in the eyes. "Haven't you ever wondered why your episodes are exactly twenty-nine days apart?"

I felt like there was an engine slowly turning in my stomach. "And there's no cure?"

"Not at this time," Siodmak said. "Some treatments have been known to reduce the duration of an episode, but nothing is conclusive yet."

"Does Diana know?" I asked.

Siodmark nodded.

"Then why didn't she tell me?" I almost growled.

"Would you have believed her if she did?" Siodmark shot back. "Every case is different. We've seen relationships torn apart over this. That's why we have the treatment, so everyone can see for themselves in a controlled environment."

I didn't say anything at first. I just nodded on, lost in thought about my situation.

"But there is research to find a cure?" I said. Siodmak nodded firmly.

"Yes. It's costing a ton to keep this disease out of the headlines for fear of starting a panic every month. Quite a lot of money is being spent on clinical research and development," the doctor explained.

"Do you know if they need a lab rat?" I asked.

"I will make some calls," Siodmak said. "I am almost certain they need fresh volunteers. But I can't make any promises on the results."

"Thanks Doc," I said.

"Matthews will see you to your room," Siodmak said with a brief smile. Matthews appeared at my side.

"You ready to go?" Mathews asked. I nodded as I returned to the squeaky wheelchair.

"By the way, your aim was way off last night. Aren't you supposed to shoot the monster in the heart? You didn't even come close," I snorted.

"I was aiming for your mouth. Figured it was the best way to shut you up," Matthews scoffed.

That night, I called Diana and apologized. In the end, we were both crying. We agreed to start meeting for dinner on Wednesdays.

I popped off the end of the permanent marker. The thick, odorous scent of the ink breezed into my nostrils. I looked back at the calendar, marker in hand. I could tell Big Lycanthropy what I told prostate cancer before chemo, and what I told my third heart attack before triple bypass surgery.

Bring it on.
One day without incident.
Twenty-eight more to go.

You can follow us:

on **Twitter** (@WyldbloodPress)
on **Facebook** (www.facebook.com/WyldboodPress)
on our **website** (www.wyldblood.com)
or by subscribing to our **newsletter**
(http://eepurl.com/haa4Zn).